Colin Marveled At The Tiny Baby He Had Helped Bring Into The World.

Her fingers were doubled into small fists, her arms thrown up over her head while she slept propped on her side. He touched her soft cheek, wondering about her, imagining a little girl with long red hair and big green eyes, a tiny version of Katherine. He felt a tightening in his chest.

He turned and looked at Katherine. She was on her back, one arm flung out, her red hair spilling over her shoulders. His gaze traveled over the hospital gown, the sheet that was across her hips and legs. He drew a deep breath. All his tender feelings stirred by the sight of the baby were transformed to desire for the sleeping woman.

He moved to a chair, placing it closer to the bassinet, not trusting himself to sit too close to Katherine. He propped his booted feet on a table, settled back and closed his eyes....

Dear Reader,

This month: strong and sexy heroes!

First, the Tallchiefs—that intriguing, legendary family—are back, and this time it's Birk Tallchief who meets his match in Cait London's MAN OF THE MONTH, *The Groom Candidate*. Birk's been pining for Lacey MacCandliss for years, but once he gets her, there's nothing but trouble of the most *romantic* kind. Don't miss this delightful story from one of Desire's most beloved writers.

Next, nobody creates a strong, sexy hero quite like Sara Orwig, and in her latest, *Babes in Arms,* she brings us Colin Whitefeather, a tough and tender man you'll never forget. And in Judith McWilliams's *Another Man's Baby* we meet Philip Lysander, a Greek tycoon who will do anything to save his family...even pretend to be a child's father.

Peggy Moreland's delightful miniseries, TROUBLE IN TEXAS, continues with *Lone Star Kind of Man*. The man in question is rugged rogue cowboy Cody Fipes. In *Big Sky Drifter*, by Doreen Owens Malek, a wild Wyoming man named Cal Winston tames a lonely woman. And in Cathie Linz's *Husband Needed*, bachelor Jack Elliott surprises himself when he offers to trade his single days for married nights.

In Silhouette Desire you'll always find the most irresistible men around! So enjoy!

Lucia Macro

Senior Editor

Please address questions and book requests to:
Silhouette Reader Service
U.S.: 3010 Walden Ave., P.O. Box 1325, Buffalo, NY 14269
Canadian: P.O. Box 609, Fort Erie, Ont. L2A 5X3

SARA
ORWIG
BABES IN ARMS

SILHOUETTE *Desire*®
Published by Silhouette Books
America's Publisher of Contemporary Romance

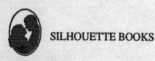

SILHOUETTE BOOKS

ISBN 0-373-76094-9

BABES IN ARMS

Copyright © 1997 by Sara Orwig

Printed in U.S.A.

Books by Sara Orwig

Silhouette Desire

Falcon's Lair #938
The Bride's Choice #1019
A Baby for Mommy #1060
Babes in Arms #1094

Silhouette Intimate Moments

Hide in Plain Sight #679

SARA ORWIG

lives with her husband and children in Oklahoma. She has a patient husband who will take her on research trips anywhere from big cities to old forts. She is an avid collector of Western history books. With a master's degree in English, Sara writes historical romance, mainstream fiction and contemporary romance. Books are beloved treasures that take Sara to magical worlds, and she loves both reading and writing them.

With thanks to Lucia Macro, Lynda Curnyn,
Cathleen Treacy, Tina Colombo and Maureen Walters.

One

"**Y**ou can pick up your check from Della. Thanks again on this last case," Abe Swenson, the red-haired Payne County sheriff said. "You know if you ever want to go full-time with us—"

"Sorry," Colin interrupted him. "As an honorary deputy I more freedom, and I'm enjoying ranching." He didn't add that every time he took on police work, he swore it would be the last.

"You better head home soon. I've been getting weather bulletins. Highways are closing all across the northern and eastern part of the state. Our bus terminal closed twenty minutes ago."

Colin nodded. "Old Blue does pretty well in snow."

"Yeah, well, we may have an ice storm before tonight."

"Thanks, Abe." Colin stopped by the desk, flirting a moment with Della while she gave him his check. He pulled his shearling coat closed, jammed his black Stetson on his head and pushed open the glass door.

Snow swirled and fell silently, coating sidewalks, frosting the yellow dried Bermuda grass, turning to slush in the streets. Striding to the bed of a battered robin's-egg-blue pickup, he adjusted the tarp over the sacks of groceries piled in the back and then climbed inside, moving into the Friday afternoon traffic. He headed down Sixth toward the university. Bumper-to-bumper student traffic slowed him to a creeping pace.

He turned onto the strip, moving past shops, beer parlors and restaurants, watching two guys throw snowballs at three pretty coeds, feeling a moment's pang of loneliness, which was gone as swiftly as it came.

He crept to the next light and slowed as the yellow switched to red. To his right at the curb across the intersection, a woman stepped out of a car. She closed and locked the car and glanced up and down the street. Taller than average, yet looking thick through the middle in her bulky hip-length brown parka, she had a wrinkled gray cap pulled over her head, owlish glasses perched on her nose and baggy jeans. She carried a bulky leather bag held over her shoulder by a strap.

The woman dashed across the side street against traffic, crossing in spite of the light. A car slid on the snow and honked at her as she turned to cross the street in front of Colin. She glanced his way and he gazed into wide green eyes. Beneath the gray cap, her hair was pulled back into a bun. She reached the curb and disappeared into a bookstore.

"Stupid broad," Colin muttered. He adjusted the rearview mirror. Behind him in the next block two men in black topcoats climbed out of a shiny car and hurried toward the bookstore.

Overdressed for the day, the men were not typical of the small university town, and Colin's cop's instinct kicked in as he remembered the wide-eyed look the woman had given him.

"You're imagining things, Whitefeather," he said aloud to himself while the light changed. He shifted and drove on, looking at the two men as they walked down the street. They didn't glance to the right or left, and every instinct in him screamed *muscle*. "Stay out of it."

He hunched over the wheel, listening to the clack of the wipers when he turned in front of the fire station and glimpsed the campus. Snow bathed it in pristine beauty, the red brick of Old Central looking warm and solid, its green cupola at the peak of the roof still showing beneath an icing of snow. Boughs of evergreens draped in white dipped earthward and students clad in bright parkas reminded Colin of colorful birds as they crossed the sprawling campus.

"Oh, hell," Colin said, signaling at the next corner and circling the block. "You'll stick your nose where it doesn't belong," he grumbled to himself, yet he couldn't get the woman's face out of his mind, the big eyes that looked frightened. Because of one-way streets, he had to drive two blocks to circle back onto Station Avenue again. As he paused at the intersection and glanced up and down, he noticed another burly man in a parka headed toward the bookstore from a block away to the south.

"Someone should give you guys a lesson in how to blend into your surroundings," Colin mumbled, shifting and swinging into traffic on Station.

It was a moment before he spotted her walking toward him on the right side of the street. Except for her height, she would have faded into the crowd. The two topcoats were striding toward her from the north end of the street, so she was boxed in.

A voice inside him, screaming to stay out of it, lost its battle as Colin swung the car closer to the curb and threw open the door on the passenger side. "Get in. I'm a cop and I'll get you away from them."

Her big eyes focused on him and for an instant he forgot the danger and felt lost in depths of green. The moment became timeless. He became conscious of everything around him, the noise of car engines, the swishing sounds of tires in slush, the swirling snow. She stared back, an unwavering, probing look that narrowed the world into an awareness of just her. Other sounds and sights faded from his mind as he stared at her with as much intensity as if she had reached out and touched him.

Then she shook her head, her eyes widening while she glanced around, reminding him of a trapped animal. The topcoats had increased their pace and were only half a block away. When Colin looked at her again, she was entering a restaurant. Colin slammed the door and drove past the two men as they rushed toward the restaurant.

Ignoring gut feelings to stay out of her problem, he turned at the corner and signaled, swinging into the alley. He guessed right. She emerged from the back of the restaurant and hurried toward him. He opened the door again.

"I'm telling the truth. I am a cop."

She glanced over her shoulder as the two men stepped into the alley. With a swirl of her coat, she climbed into the pickup and slammed the door. Telling himself he was every kind of fool, Colin threw the pickup into reverse while a faint, sweet scent of roses filled the interior.

As soon as the pickup rolled out of the alley into the street Colin accelerated, taking the next corner without slowing. He fished his billfold out and flipped it open, turning to the badge that he carried.

"Here," he said, tossing the open billfold into her lap. He turned another corner, sped several blocks down a street and went through an alley. Emerging from the alley, he whipped around the corner, speeding along more streets and alleys until he braked in the middle of an alley and turned into a small garage.

"What are you doing?" Her voice was low and filled with alarm, the drawl of the South softening the r's in her speech.

"Losing them. I'm covering our tracks. Just a minute," he said, taking the keys and climbing out to push the garage door closed. Two windows in the garage allowed dim light as Colin climbed back into the pickup. Silence enveloped them.

"Tracks into this garage will show," she said, sounding terrified. She had unbuckled her seat belt and was against the door, her gloved fingers on the handle as if she were ready to run.

"After another five minutes our tracks will be obliterated. The flakes are big now and coming down fast."

Katherine Manchester was frightened, yet wanted to trust him. If only he weren't a policeman. And if only he weren't so big. She eyed his broad shoulders, covered by the shearling coat. He filled the interior of the pickup. One look at his long legs, folded in the narrow space, and she knew he was a tall man. She met a direct brown-eyed gaze that studied her with enough intensity to make her nervous. "Do you live here?"

"No, this isn't my home. A friend lives here and he's on duty now, so he won't be home. We'll sit here for a few minutes. I'm Colin Whitefeather."

She hesitated, debating whether to give him her real name or not. When she didn't answer right away, she noticed his eyes narrowed. "I'm Katherine Manchester," she said carefully, giving her real name and watching him to see if there was any recognition. To her relief, his expression didn't change.

"Welcome to Stillwater, Katherine," Colin said in a friendly tone, and Katherine felt as if something inside her was loosening. She fought against the feeling, knowing she didn't dare relax. The man was a cop, for heaven's sake, even if it was only honorary! His long, shaggy hair gave him a wild appearance, and his broad shoulders beneath the thick coat gave an aura of power and command that frightened her, yet at the same time, so far, he had been only kind and helpful. Almost too good to be true, and she waited warily.

"Just a minute." Colin climbed out and untied the tarp, rummaging in sacks and finding a package of cookies, a sack of apples and a carton of milk. He climbed back into the truck and held the groceries out to her. "Here are some snacks."

"Thank you," she said, taking them. She pulled out a tissue to polish and clean the apples, handing one to him.

"They'll watch your car," Colin stated quietly.

Chewing a bite of apple, her gaze returned to him. "Is there an airport or bus station here?"

"The commercial flights are grounded and the bus station closed a little while ago because of the storm," he answered, seeing a flicker of worry in her eyes. Was she just going to abandon the car? As he stared at her, looking at prominent cheekbones, a straight nose and full lips that made a man fantasize, he realized she was trying to hide her beauty. Her face was covered with thick makeup, her eyebrows penciled to look heavier. For the first time, he spotted the red roots to the mousy brown hair. She had tried to change her appearance and he realized that she had downplayed her looks, smudging makeup beneath her eyes, trying to change the shape of her brows and mouth. As he looked at her dowdy, nondescript clothing, he remembered her shiny black car.

He glanced again at the red roots, imagining glossy red hair. He suspected she was tall and willowy and a real looker—with heavy muscle after her. He wondered about

Las Vegas and a mob. She was someone's girlfriend or she had stolen something or knew something. For the kind of muscle involved and her obvious fear, money had to be part of her flight. The purse was kept constantly at her fingertips and he guessed she was packing a pistol.

She opened the carton of milk, taking a long drink, and Colin wondered when she had last eaten.

The faint rumble of a car motor grew louder. Even beneath the heavy makeup, her face paled. She stopped chewing, inhaling swiftly, and he had the feeling that she was holding her breath. Her hand clutched the purse until her knuckles were white. She wore no rings on her slender fingers with short, neatly clipped nails. The sound of the motor increased. A car was slowly creeping along the alley.

Colin reached behind his back beneath his jacket to withdraw the 9 mm automatic pistol he carried tucked into his waistband. He watched the door of the garage.

"Maybe you should get down until they're gone," he said, trying to keep his voice casual. He glanced in the rearview mirror while she slid down on the floor.

The low growl of a motor went past and faded. As Colin replaced his pistol, he jerked his head. "It's gone," he said, and she moved awkwardly back onto the seat.

"We'll wait a while before we leave here."

"You can let me out somewhere on campus."

"They'll be watching your car and probably the bus station, even though it's closed. There's no train."

She ran a hand over her eyes and turned to stare at the snow-covered garage window. "Have you heard a weather report?"

"The storm is supposed to get worse. I have to head northeast from here. My ranch is several miles from town. I can take you to Pawnee and you can get a bus out of there to Tulsa, where you can get a plane."

White teeth caught a full underlip and he inhaled as he stared at her rosy mouth, a sudden curiosity plaguing him over what it would be like to feel the softness of her full lips. *Crazy notion,* an inner voice cautioned. The lady was pure trouble, the kind he did not need. He had already volunteered to drive to Pawnee in a blinding blizzard, which meant he could get snowbound in Pawnee or be until nightfall getting home.

"Thank you, but if you'll just let me out on campus, I'll manage."

Let her out and tell her goodbye. "You won't get out of town. This is too small a place to get lost easily, and they'll find you," he persisted, wondering if he was losing his wits. He ought to be thankful she wanted to be rid of him. And she wasn't reassured by his badge—that opened more questions, and again he thought of a Vegas showgirl who might know too much for her own good. Except this one didn't look like a showgirl. Far from it. Or she could be carrying money in the purse. Or drugs. There was a thought, Whitefeather, he told himself with a silent, cynical sneer.

"I think I can manage," she persisted, and he let it drop. Get rid of the woman because she could only be trouble. She'd made her choice.

They sat in silence for a few minutes and then she opened the chocolate cookies carefully and offered him one which he took. He ate a cookie, watching her bite daintily into one and chew, the tip of her pink tongue flicking out to catch a tiny crumb of chocolate on her lower lip and suddenly he wanted to lean forward and taste her mouth, chocolate and all. What was it about her that stirred the erotic thoughts? With her unattractive clothes and heavy makeup, he should barely give her a thought, yet the woman stirred him in the most basic male way. Disgruntled, he shifted in the seat to look at the garage door and glance again at his watch.

"You're a policeman and a rancher?"

"A rancher and an honorary deputy. The sheriff hires me occasionally. I prefer ranching. It's more peaceful."

She looked as if she doubted what he was saying, and he wondered again what kind of trouble she was in.

He glanced at his watch and opened the door. "It's probably been long enough. The bad thing—my pickup is noticeable, but there are two others in town as blue as this one."

He opened the garage door, backed out and closed it again.

As soon as he slid behind the wheel, she turned to him. "The garage door was open when we came."

"It was closed when that car drove down the alley. I'll tell my friend I was here and closed it." As Colin turned onto the street, he couldn't spot any black car cruising nearby. "Want out any particular place on campus? The Union will have the most people going in and out."

"Fine," she said, clutching the purse tightly again.

He drove six blocks before he had to turn onto a street where traffic was heavy. While snow swirled and the wipers clacked like a slow metronome, they inched along. Colin wiped the steamed windows with the back of his gloved hand. He glanced into the rearview mirror and saw a black car come out of a parking lot and turn into traffic two blocks behind him. He drove two more blocks and turned left. In seconds he saw the black car moving into the line of cars behind him.

"This isn't your day," he said quietly. "I think we picked up a tail."

Two

He turned at the next two corners, drove a block and looked back to see the black car turn on the same street, now three cars behind him. He glanced at her. "Still want out at the Union?"

She bit her lower lip again, and he wondered if she had any idea that something so casual could be so sexy. Maybe she was a high-priced call girl on the run, accustomed to stirring men. He rejected that thought immediately, when he remembered her reluctance to go with him and the fear in her expression when he had driven into the garage and cut the motor. She was far too afraid of him to be a hooker.

Without signaling he turned abruptly, circling the block. As he glanced in the mirror, he saw the black car move into traffic two cars behind him again. "I can lose them and take you to Pawnee or let you out near the Union, but they're less than a block behind us."

He heard her draw a deep breath. When he glanced at

her she was looking out the window, her head turned. A stray wisp of brown hair had escaped her cap and curled on her shoulder.

"Or I can take you to the police. They'll protect you," he offered.

"No!" The emphatic answer was instant, and he glanced at her. She bit her lip and looked away quickly, but not fast enough that he hadn't seen fear in her eyes again. His curiosity mushroomed. Why did she want to avoid the police?

"If you don't mind, I'll go to Pawnee," she said, as if he had asked her if she would like a trip to prison.

You got yourself into this. Looking at the tumbling snow, he gripped the steering wheel. Now he had to drive to Pawnee in a blizzard. *What had she done to cause such a hunt?* And why did she cause him to fall all over himself trying to help her?

For a second he was tempted to go to the station and turn her over to the force and let the law answer the questions. The law would protect her from the topcoats and the police would find out why she was running. Colin glanced at her profile and decided he would take her to Pawnee.

Pressing the accelerator, Colin raced into an alley, sliding and skidding as he turned out of it and doubled back, winding through alleys and down less traveled streets to the campus. At the animal-science building he jumped the curb to drive between two buildings, the college kids laughing as he bounced down into the street and sped away before the campus police were called.

He wound through town for twenty minutes and then he took a section line into the country. With satisfaction he glanced in the rearview mirror and saw the road behind him was a swirling white emptiness. He slowed and relaxed, taking the highway.

The first peppering of sleet was as faint as pebbles spilling on a sidewalk, but in seconds the hissing and staccato clicks drowned out the noise of the pickup's ancient engine.

"Katherine, we can't get to Pawnee. In this I'll be lucky to get home. I can get good traction in the snow, but nothing has traction on ice." He glanced at her and was startled by the distrust in her eyes.

"I'm safe for you to be with. If I weren't, I could have done something back there in the garage," he stated quietly. Even though she nodded, he could feel her reluctance and her fear.

"I take groceries to my folks. They have a place next door to mine. It won't take long, but I have to stop there," he said, wondering if meeting his parents would reassure her.

"Fine," she replied, and her voice was impassive.

"Where are you from?" he asked. "Tennessee?"

"I was born in Virginia, but I've moved a lot since then. Is Oklahoma your home?"

"Yes," he replied, noticing she had avoided giving him an answer. "My parents are Comanche and my family has been here since my ancestors were sent to Indian Territory. I lived in Missouri for a long time after college, but my folks have always lived in Oklahoma."

"Are you married?" she asked him and he shook his head.

"My wife died. Are you married?"

"No," she answered, locking her gloved fingers together in her lap.

They lapsed into silence and the only sounds were the rumble of the motor, the clack of windshield wipers and the drumming of sleet, which had become fine bits of ice again.

The world was a white blur, cedar limbs sagging under the weight of snow topped with ice. Lines and trees spar-

kled as ice coated thin branches and wires. A rabbit dashed
from the bar ditch, racing across the road.

Katherine felt chilled to the bone, even though the heater
was keeping the interior of the pickup toasty warm. She
glanced surreptitiously at the dark-haired man driving the
pickup. He had gotten them out of Stillwater, but was she
headed for something worse? A cop was about the last
person she wanted to encounter, much less trust with her
life. And this man looked strong and tough. She glanced
at his hands on the steering wheel, looking at the straight,
blunt fingers, well-shaped but large hands. She could imagine the hurt they might inflict.

The pickup bounced across a cattle guard, rumbling over
the rise and slowing as Colin headed for a house nestled
beneath tall bare-limbed cottonwoods and bushy snow-
covered cedars. A streamer of white smoke wafted from a
large chimney. "This won't take long. Come inside and
meet my folks."

"I'll wait here." How dangerous could he be when he
had his parents within miles? She knew too well that parents weren't a guarantee against violence in grown sons.

Ignoring her protest, Colin Whitefeather squared his
black Stetson on his head, and went around to open her
door. Long limbed, at least four inches over six feet tall,
his dark skin and dark hair gave him a touch of wildness,
as if he spent his time outdoors dealing with the elements.
His shoulders were broad, his hands big, and he frightened
her, but he was the only hope she had at the moment.

When he closed the car door behind her, he stepped to
the back. As he yanked free the ties of the tarp and swept
snow to the ground with his arm, a tall, striking woman
opened the back door. Waving at them, she had the same
prominent cheekbones and dark eyes as her son. Colin
picked up two sacks of groceries and handed them to Kath-

erine, taking three more in his arms and hurrying to the house.

Determined to get ahead of Katherine, Colin crossed the yard in long strides.

"Did you have difficulty getting here?" his mother asked, her dark brown gaze going beyond him to Katherine.

He leaned forward to brush his mother's cheek with a kiss. "Don't ask questions, Mom. I don't know her and she's in trouble." He stepped onto the back porch and stomped snow off his black western boots and turned as Katherine entered.

"Mom, this is Katherine Manchester. Katherine, this is my mother, Nadine Whitefeather."

"Come in. I have hot chocolate ready."

"Mom, it's icing up out there. We should get home while we can."

"You can drink hot chocolate," she said firmly, leading the way into the roomy kitchen with glass-fronted cabinets.

"I thought I heard voices," Will Whitefeather said, entering the room.

Katherine faced a man only a few inches shorter than Colin and even more broad in the shoulders. Will Whitefeather looked sturdy and strong enough to lift the front of the blue pickup off the ground. His dark skin was lined and creased from the weather, yet as he smiled at her there was something reassuring about him that made her want to drop her guard. And then she remembered how gullible she had been in the past, how pulled into danger she was now.

"Dad, this is Katherine Manchester. Katherine, meet my father, Will Whitefeather."

"We're glad to have you, even though it's a terrible day to be out," Will said openly and to her relief, her name seemed to mean nothing to any of the Whitefeather family.

"Sit down, Katherine, while I put away groceries," Colin said. "Mom will be back in a minute and pour the hot chocolate and then, Dad, I'll help you break the ice and feed the livestock."

"If you need to get home, Colin, you go on. It's getting slick and I just heard a weather report. We're supposed to get more ice and six inches of snow."

"I'll take your coat." Colin Whitefeather stepped behind her, waiting while Katherine unfastened the wrinkled parka. He slipped it off her shoulders and hung it on a peg, turning to motion toward the kitchen chairs. "Have a seat," he said, his gaze going over her fuzzy purple sweater, which hung to her knees. Shock immobilized him momentarily, now that the bulky coat no longer hid her figure. Katherine Manchester looked six months pregnant.

Aware of his gaze going swiftly over her figure, she felt a flush of embarrassment. Self-consciously she removed her hat; she could imagine how terrible her hair looked. She had put it up in the early hours of the morning and worn the cap all day and she could feel locks that had tumbled loose from the braids. When she handed him her hat, her fingers brushed his in a casual touch that should have been unnoticed, yet the contact stirred a tingling current.

As Katherine turned around, Colin's dark gaze was on her, studying her features, and her self-consciousness increased. She never intended anyone to scrutinize her so closely. She stared into his dark eyes, conscious of him as a male, too aware of an electric tension snapping between them. Her pulse jumped and then surprise shook her, because she couldn't recall reacting to a man in such a manner since she was twenty years old.

He turned away to shed his coat and her pulse took another lurch, because beneath the bulky coat he was broad shouldered and slim hipped, a red wool shirt tucked into faded jeans that molded long legs.

He shook his shaggy black hair away from his face and crossed the kitchen to help his father, the two bearing a close resemblance in their rugged facial planes, the arrogant hawklike noses and strong jaws.

Trying to ignore Colin Whitefeather, Katherine glanced around the room, which was filled with a clutter of appliances and tempting smells coming from the oven. The aroma of hot chocolate wafted on the air, wrapping around her like a cloak, making her remember moments of her childhood when life had been predictable. Cheerful yellow-and-white curtains were tied back at the frosted windows and thriving green plants hung from hooks. Katherine felt momentarily safe and wished she could politely thank Colin Whitefeather and stay here with his parents until the snow thawed.

"One cup, Mom, and then I'll help Dad and we'll be on our way," Colin said good-naturedly while his mother poured steaming cups of hot chocolate. He leaned back in the chair, stretching out his long legs, and Katherine thought how strong and reliable he looked. Yet she knew far too well how deceiving looks could be.

"You don't have far to go and you'll manage it." Nadine smiled at Katherine.

Colin sipped his hot chocolate as Katherine raised her mug to her lips. The thick pottery mug warmed her fingers and the steaming chocolate tasted delicious, the first hot food in too long.

"Dad, we need to get going as soon as we can. I want to get the chores done," Colin said, standing and carrying his mug of chocolate to the counter.

"Let's go," Will answered, pulling on a heavy coat and jamming a battered wide-brimmed hat on his head.

As the men left, Nadine moved around the kitchen

cleaning cups and pouring more hot chocolate. After ten minutes of listening to Nadine talk about recipes and Colin when he was a child, Katherine realized that Nadine had not asked her a single question about her life, and she wondered if Colin had said something or if Nadine simply had her thoughts on her own family.

Dreading leaving with Colin again, Katherine still felt tense, watching the clock until finally she heard the slap of the door to the porch and the men's voices and foot-stomping. Colin thrust his head inside. "Katherine, if you'll get your coat, I won't even come inside, because it's sleeting again."

She moved across the kitchen to put on her coat. Wiping her hands on a towel, Nadine Whitefeather followed her. "I'm glad you stopped by with Colin. Sometimes I worry about him being alone."

"He won't be alone tonight," Katherine said, looking at the sleet that was laying a sheet of ice over the snow.

"Here, take this," Nadine urged, thrusting a warm sealed plastic container into Katherine's hands. "It's chili. Colin can cook, but he has a limited menu."

"Thank you, Mrs. Whitefeather," Katherine said, turning to look at his mother. "It was nice to have met you."

"It was nice to meet you, Katherine. I hope things work out for you."

"Thank you," Katherine repeated, startled and realizing Colin must have said something about her to his mother when they first arrived. She opened the back door and crossed the porch, seeing Colin waiting.

As they stepped off the porch, she slid on the ice. Instantly Colin Whitefeather's arm went around her waist to steady her. His arm was a strong band, nothing more than a friendly, helpful gesture, yet a chilly withdrawal gripped her.

"Thanks," she said, trying not to stiffen and make him

aware of her reaction. "I'll be all right," she said, pulling away. He took her arm firmly and she had to fight the urge to shake free of his grip.

In minutes they were back in the truck, the chili on the seat between them. "Your folks are very nice," she said quietly, her nervousness increasing at the thought of being shut away in a blizzard with a total stranger who was a strong male and a cop.

"I moved back to Oklahoma so I can help Dad, although he doesn't need me often. The men who work for me help out over here, too."

Riding in silence, they crept to the section line and then turned east and Katherine couldn't see any road. They were going little over ten miles an hour and the sleet was still coming down.

"Lines will be down in this one," Colin said, wiping the windshield with the back of his hand. Seemingly in the middle of nowhere, the truck bounced over a cattle guard. He slowed to a halt and climbed out.

"Be right back. Want to close the gate," he shouted and slammed the door while a flurry of white flakes tumbled over the car seat and melted.

Turning around, she wiped the window and saw he was swinging closed a large gate and padlocking it. Without a word he climbed back into the truck and put it into gear, driving slowly. They crept through an endlessly white world with a blinding lack of color and snow-covered objects that mesmerized and confused.

She shivered, wondering about his past, worrying about the present. She would be alone with him, miles from anyone, caught in a storm. She shivered and rubbed her arms, telling herself to stop being such an idiot.

Finally through the tumbling snow the darker bulk of a building loomed up. As they drove closer, she saw the house and attached garage. Pressing the garage-door opener, he waited while the door slid open. Fear wrapped around her more tightly than the coat she pulled close.

They entered a three-car garage that had an empty space, a Jeep and a space for the pickup. The noise of sleet hitting the truck dimmed to a staccato sound peppering the garage roof.

When the engine died, Colin climbed out. With a mounting reluctance, Katherine slowly opened the pickup door. They were in a large garage that adjoined a house. A black shadow dashed from a corner, followed by a great, shaggy gray dog. She gasped, her heart thudding and then calming as Colin Whitefeather turned to pet the animals. "This is Buster. The wolf is Lobo."

She was still in the pickup and she eyed the dogs. "He's really a wolf?" she asked, trying to take time to deal with her fear. The animal had to be a wolf. She gazed into yellow predator eyes. He had long legs and thick gray fur and his ears cocked forward as he studied her. "You're certain it's safe for me to get out? They look ferocious."

"They're lambs. And they know if I brought you in my car, you're my guest." He gave a short whistle and both dogs trotted to him. He petted them a few seconds. "Sit."

Both animals sat down. "They won't bite. I promise."

She climbed out of the pickup. "They don't have to sit. I'm just on edge." She patted her knee as an invitation to them.

"Good dogs," he said and they ran to her to mill around her. Katherine petted them, scratching their ears. "They're beautiful animals."

"Buster is a Border collie and Lobo is just what his name implies. I found him when he was a pup and I was up north. He was hurt and I brought him home with me."

"So you take in strays often, Colin Whitefeather," she remarked, giving him a faint smile.

He shook his head. "You two are it," he said, gathering sacks into his arms.

Doubting his last remark, she picked up the chili and a sack of groceries and followed Colin inside a kitchen that was much newer than his parents' kitchen. Buster ran past them and stood near an empty dog dish. Lobo came inside to sit and watch Colin. The cozy kitchen held a huge fireplace built with large slabs of sandstone. Knotty-pine cabinets lined the walls. The kitchen formed an L-shaped room with the living area, which had bookcases, a pair of navy wing chairs, a maroon-and-navy sofa and another huge stone fireplace. The living area was paneled in pine, with louvered shutters at the windows. Beneath beamed ceilings, the room held the same cozy, rustic, masculine look as the kitchen.

"Make yourself at home," Colin said, setting groceries on a long oak table. "There's only one bedroom," he added with a shrug, "but that sofa makes into a bed."

Colin hung his coat on a peg by the door, motioning to her to do the same. "As soon as I light a fire in here and put away the groceries, I'll give you a tour so you'll know where everything is," he said.

When she removed her coat, Katherine felt stiff and cold and wary. She watched while Colin Whitefeather put away his groceries, seeming to ignore her as if he had forgotten her presence, and she found his lack of attention to her reassuring, yet she was afraid to let down her guard.

He picked up a phone and after a few moments she gathered he must be talking to his ranch foreman. She hadn't given much thought to other men on the place.

"Bud," Colin said, "tell the others that I locked the gate and I'll turn on the alarm tonight. I brought a guest home with me, and some guys are after her. They look dangerous," he said, finally turning to give her a level look.

It sounded worse to hear him talk about the men after her.

"If any of you see strangers, be careful and get word to me at once. They're armed, so the men better be prepared. Any shooting starts, call 911 as quickly as you can."

She rubbed her arms, wondering how many men she had placed in danger by coming home with him.

"Sure, I will. No one can get through in this. I let the dogs out. Good. Thanks. See you in the morning." He replaced the receiver.

"I've brought danger to you and to others," she said quietly.

"I want them to be aware of the danger, but they can take good care of themselves and those goons aren't after any cowboys. Don't worry about it."

As if he had dismissed the whole thing from his mind, he squatted in front of the fireplace to stack logs for a fire. She watched him work and knew she should relax. The man was ignoring her most of the time, but she couldn't let down her guard.

"C'mon," he said when a fire blazed. "Tour time." He left the kitchen and she followed, keeping her purse at her side, feeling wary of him even though he sounded pleasant.

He led her down a wide hall and he motioned at an open door. "Here's the one bathroom," he said. "Towels are in the cabinet."

She glanced inside, aware she had to move within inches of him. She peeked into a room done in maroon-and-navy decor with an old-fashioned footed tub and an open door to her left that probably led to his bedroom.

She was aware of standing too close to Colin White-feather. He was a tall man, tall enough to make her look up when she gazed into his eyes, something that she rarely had to do with any man. Even Sloan was only inches taller than she.

Colin's size added to her nervousness because she felt vulnerable. He was broad shouldered, long armed and powerful. She glanced at the bathroom and moved away quickly.

Colin led the way through the open door at the end of the hall. "Here's my room, and I wasn't expecting company."

When she stepped inside, her attention was caught by the panoramic view through large windows and glass doors that opened onto a deck. Snow fell in big, tumbling flakes and the countryside looked like a Christmas-card scene. She glanced around the room at the king-sized bed with rumpled covers, jeans tossed on a chair, a shirt draped on a television set. Fishing poles were in a corner and boots kicked off on the floor in the middle of the room.

The bedroom had the same pine paneling and the same navy-and-maroon decor as the rest of the house. A potted plant in the corner had one of his ties draped over it.

"I'm not compulsively neat," he said, flashing a grin. Katherine's heart missed a beat because the smile gave him a come-hither appeal. Creases lined his tanned cheeks and his teeth were white against his dark skin, the grin softening the harshness of his features. And she was surprised at herself and her reaction to his smile. Until this moment, she would have bet all the money in her purse that she would not find any male appealing for a long time.

"I'm glad to be in out of the storm. I don't mind the clutter," she replied, turning away from him.

"This is it, my small castle. Let's get Mom's chili on the stove. Do you eat chili?" Colin asked, aware she was still clutching her purse tightly, pressing it against her side beneath her arm. He remembered a skittish colt that he had purchased. The animal was terrified of anyone coming

within yards of him and Colin suspected the former owner
had beaten the animal badly. It had taken a long time to
calm the colt and to finally turn him into a riding horse.

"Yes. It smelled wonderful at your mother's."

In minutes they had both washed up and Katherine
moved around the kitchen, tearing greens into a bowl for
salad while Colin reheated Nadine's chili. Katherine
worked silently, and Colin noticed she was never too far
from her purse. Once when her back was turned, he picked
it up, feeling the heft of it and deciding she was packing
a pistol.

Colin's gaze shifted back to Katherine, and he wondered
about the hair pulled up and pinned close to her head,
wisps escaping the pins to wave slightly over her ears and
her slender neck. Diamond stud earrings were in her ears,
but she wore no other jewelry. Since they arrived at his
house she seemed tense, and he suspected if he made a
sudden noise, she would jump a foot into the air.

They sat down to eat over steaming bowls of chili, hot
corn tortillas and bowls of green salad. They ate in silence
for a few minutes.

He wondered again if she was a showgirl, yet she was
a long way from Vegas or Reno. Someone with money
was involved, for three men to be after her.

Colin glanced at the darkened windows, feeling safe
with the storm raging outside. Where were the men now
who were after her today? In a Stillwater motel? In this
storm they couldn't scour the countryside, so they had to
be holed up somewhere.

Colin stretched out his arm and picked up the television
remote control. "We might as well have the television on
in the background."

"Do you mind if we don't?" she asked hastily, her eyes
wide and fear plain in their green depths. His gaze locked
with hers while the air seemed to crackle with tension be-

tween them. A log fell in the fire, yet all of Colin's attention focused on the woman facing him. Her lashes fluttered and she turned away abruptly.

Studying her, he placed the remote control on the table with deliberation. "You don't want to go to the cops. You don't want the television on. Maybe it's time you tell me a little about the trouble you're in."

Three

___

Katherine's heart lurched. She had expected him to quiz her more when she first climbed into the pickup with him. But gradually, as the hours passed, she had stopped worrying. Sitting attentive and still, he was waiting for her answer. Awareness that he was a lawman made her blood run cold. As far as she knew, Sloan had not gone to the police to get her back, but that could change at any time.

Stalling for a moment while she decided how to answer, she sipped ice water and wiped the corners of her mouth with her fingers, staring down at her plate. "I'm divorced now, but I had an abusive husband."

"If you're divorced, why do you still fear him?"

Lies swirled in her mind, stories that might satisfy Colin, but one look into his alert brown eyes and she decided to tell him the truth. "I'm pregnant and my ex-husband wants me back."

"He wants his baby?"

"It's my baby," Katherine replied fiercely, and then realized how she had snapped her answer at him. "I'll be gone tomorrow, so why don't we just leave it at that," she suggested, holding her breath and praying he would stop questioning her.

"Look, you had three pros chasing you," Colin replied with an obvious note of impatience in his tone. "That's big muscle with money and power behind it. I've given you shelter and run a risk. I'd like to know just how big a risk I'm taking here. I'm not going to run and call your ex-husband, but I want to know what I'm up against as long as I have you under my roof."

"It shouldn't matter. I'll be gone as soon as the snow stops, and they can't get to us until it stops."

"Katherine, I can imagine all sorts of scenarios. If you know about someone's million-dollar fraud, if you know where a body is hidden—lots of reasons that even after you are gone, those guys might come after me. They might want to know what you told me."

"Oh, no! Oh, it's not anything like that. I have an abusive husband who wants me back badly." She could see the doubt cloud his eyes, and once again she debated what to say. Watching orange flames curl around logs, she bit her lower lip. "My name didn't mean anything to you, did it?"

"Katherine Manchester." He shook his head. "No. Should it?"

"My ex-husband is Sloan Manchester," she answered cautiously.

The name struck a chord, and Colin tried to remember where he had heard it. "That sounds familiar," he said and memory stirred. Manchester Oil. "Louisiana. He's a political candidate. Oil and big business."

"That's right," Katherine said with resignation. "His father is Tyson Manchester of Manchester Oil. There are politicians who want Sloan to run for governor of Louisiana.''

"I wouldn't think a man running for governor could risk having his ex-wife stalked, much less gamble on taking you back against your will. There's a law against that."

"He expects them to get me and take me back without anyone knowing."

"Go to the press. Let me take you to the police."

"No!" She pushed back the chair, her eyes going wide and color draining from her face as she stood.

Katherine seemed ready to bolt in spite of the storm. Colin stood and reached out to take her shoulders. She flinched and jumped away from him, her hands going up to shield herself.

"Hey, hey!" he said in a gentle voice, holding up his hands. "Calm down, Katherine. I swear I won't hurt you."

She backed away from him, biting her lower lip, and he wondered what kind of monster Sloan Manchester must be.

"Sit down and we'll talk. Just relax. I won't call the police if you don't want me to," he said, keeping his voice low, trying to bank his anger.

Her ex-husband was running for governor while Katherine was sitting in Colin's kitchen, six months pregnant with the man's baby. He was sheltering a woman on the run from one of the most powerful men in the country. Colin wondered what he had gotten himself into. He should have left her alone, he told himself. Just left her the hell alone.

"As soon as the storm abates, I'll be out of your life," she said quickly.

"Let's sit down. Want to sit in front of the fire? I can do the dishes later."

She nodded, but he noticed she didn't make a move toward the chairs near the fire. She stood waiting, as if frightened to step in front of him. He moved around the table and went to put another log on the fire. As the wood crackled and popped, he closed the screen and turned to face her.

Looking like a lost child, the bulky purple sweater covering her, Katherine sat in a wing chair with her legs curled up beneath her.

"Are you really divorced?"

"Yes. At the time I asked for the divorce, Sloan had another woman in his life." She looked down at her hands in her lap while Colin listened. He noticed her nails were neatly clipped and she had long, slender fingers. "Sloan wasn't in the public light then. I asked for the divorce at the right time and he said yes. I got the divorce as quickly as possible. He regretted it almost instantly. It seems he wants what he can't have," she added bitterly.

"I gave up any money from him, but I had a little money left from savings and I took that with me. At the time of the divorce Sloan's parents were in Europe, or his father would have stopped him from getting the divorce. His father had political ambitions for Sloan long ago."

His back warmed by the fire, Colin moved to a wing chair, turning it to face her. If she was telling him the truth, she shouldn't be so frightened and she should go to the police and get help.

"Katherine," he said gently, fighting the urge to touch her lightly, jamming his hands into his pockets instead while fire heated his side. "If Sloan has given you a divorce, he can't force you to come back."

A look of pain crossed her features and was gone.

"He's a powerful man and his father is as well. They would bribe and pressure people to get what they want. He has friends in high places, friends at court. He's bribed people before to get what he wants in business."

"Then he sure as hell shouldn't be elected governor."

Her expression was pained. "I can't fight him. He would turn everything against me."

"It won't look good to have it come out that he's abusive or that he's trying to force you to return. If those thugs following you take you by force, that's kidnapping."

She faced him with a steady gaze. "My father was sent to prison for embezzlement. I have bad blood in my family, as Sloan has so often reminded me. We're Old South with relatives who were in the Confederacy, so I was acceptable to his parents and in certain social circles in New Orleans, but Sloan has said he can make me look like the most evil bitch from a corrupt family. Now I have the baby to consider."

As Colin swore softly, Katherine bit her lip and looked down, rubbing her arms again. He reached out to tilt her chin up, but the moment he stretched his hand out and lightly touched her, she flinched and jerked away. He put his hands into his pockets again.

"Katherine, I will never hit you," he said quietly, silently cursing Sloan Manchester. "I have never in my life hit a woman. Not even in the line of duty."

Her eyes widened as she stared at him and the fear dissipated in her expression. She bit her lip. "It's an automatic reaction."

He wanted to reach for her, to draw her into his arms and just hold her and reassure her that she was safe. The cynical side of him gave a silent laugh. Sure, Whitefeather, safe as a mouse in a building with a cat. Those three guys had not given up their hunt. The snow might slow them, but eventually they would find out who drove a blue pickup and where he lived. And they might do it in spite of the storm.

What was it about this woman that had brought out the protective instincts in him from the first moment he had seen her? She was almost as tall as he was, taller than nearly all the women he had ever known. She was independent, resourceful and capable of caring for herself. Capable of eluding the three hoods after her, so why did he have all these protective feelings on full throttle? And if she didn't stir his protective instincts, she stirred his desire, which should have been even more unlikely in her garish makeup and baggy clothing. The fuzzy sweater looked like a molting bear. And she had to be six months pregnant!

Colin rubbed the back of his neck. "I think some lawmen I know would listen to your story."

She shook her head. "Sloan's got powerful friends. You'd be surprised what he can do. I used to think I could find protection from his brutality, but everyone covered for him."

"He might not be so powerful here."

"The first thing you know, I'd be whisked right back to Louisiana and placed in an institution and the public would be told I'm ill or mentally unbalanced. Sloan would manage it. I don't want to go to the police."

"All right, no police, but I think you're making a mistake."

She shook her head stubbornly. "I know what's happened in the past when I've tried to get help."

"How do you think you'll get away from him?"

"I'm going to California where I have a friend who will help me. Sloan won't find me there. It's a matter of time. Once Sloan is defeated or elected, he'll forget about me. If he's defeated, it won't help to get me back. If he's elected without me, he won't care what I do. Right now he wants me at his side. He thinks it will give the proper image for him. And he's annoyed he can no longer control me."

"Are you really divorced from him?"

"I'm telling you the truth. Yes, I am."

"If you're divorced, it's a matter of public record and

the reporters should have already picked up on his marital status.''

''He has contacts at newspapers and he can give them a story about my mental condition. It's still early enough that he's not in the limelight yet.''

Colin Whitefeather's expression was a thundercloud that made her feel like running.

''I didn't mean to bring trouble down on you and I'll be gone tomorrow,'' she said swiftly, trying to appease his anger. ''Then those men won't bother you.'' Her pulse skittered as she watched him. He looked fierce and angry, and she had no doubts about his strength.

''They'll find out who drives a blue pickup in this area.'' The moment Colin said the words, she flinched as if he had struck her. ''They can't find us tonight. I can guarantee you that.'' His gaze flicked over her figure again. ''When's the baby due? About March or April?''

''No. Actually, the due date is next week.''

''*Next week!* You don't look that far along,'' he said bluntly.

''That's probably because of my height.''

He barely heard her answer. Anger rose in him, that she was being so careless about the coming event. ''You shouldn't be on the run. You need to be with relatives or a friend. You need to have a hospital lined up and not be racing across country with three goons chasing you.'' As a cop, he had seen too much death and destruction. He had reached a point where he treasured birth and life, feeling a quiet joy with every foal or calf dropped on his place. He wanted to shake some sense into the woman, but the last thing this woman needed was to be shaken. She needed a loving husband's strong arms and support. ''Where's your mother?''

''She died a year ago. I don't have any family. But I'll

be all right. When the time comes, I'll go to a hospital,"
she answered stubbornly.

"Have you even seen a doctor?"

"Yes, I have regularly. I go to clinics in cities where
I've traveled."

He ran his fingers through his hair. "Damn, your baby's
due—you're not carrying any clothing except whatever
you have stuffed in your big purse. What will you do for
diapers and formula? You know if those men are following
you, they'll take you and the baby back to Louisiana."

She raised her chin and defiance filled her eyes. "They
can't steal a baby out of a hospital. I'll manage. I had
hoped to get to California before the delivery. This snowstorm has complicated my life. And I thought I had lost
the men until this morning. I had planned to get a plane
today in Tulsa, to Denver, and from Denver to San Francisco. I thought I would be in California tonight."

"That's cutting it damned close. You have a friend
there?"

"Yes, Paula Kurczak, and she knows about the baby.
Paula has a little girl and she still has her baby things."

"Don't you know that babies don't always arrive on the
exact scheduled date?" He was fighting to bank his ex-
asperation with her. He should stop grilling her, but he
was shocked at her lack of preparation for the baby.

She smiled, her eyes crinkling at the corners, a dimple
appearing in her cheek, her white teeth flashing, and he
felt as if all the warmth of the room had drawn itself into
her smile. In spite of her ill-fitting clothes and garish
makeup, she looked adorable, and he could understand
why the ex-husband wanted her back.

"I'll be all right. And my baby will be all right."

"Have you had an ultrasound? Do you know whether
you're having a boy or a girl?"

"Yes and no. I did have an ultrasound and everything

was fine, but I told them I wanted to be surprised, so I don't know if it's a boy or a girl."

He stared at her in consternation. One week until her due date. "When this storm stops, if you won't go to the police, I'll drive you to Tulsa and put you on the plane to California."

"That would be nice of you," she said in a subdued voice.

"Do you want to call your friend in California?"

"Paula knows I'll be there some time this week. I told her I would call from the airport when I land."

He wondered whether there really was a friend in California, yet there was no big reason to lie to him. He barely knew the woman. He shouldn't care. One week until her delivery date. That revelation gave him more jitters than the thugs had. Babies had their own schedules.

"Want a refill of hot chocolate? There's more on the stove," he said, trying to defuse the moment and calm his own nerves.

"Yes, that tasted good."

She followed him into the kitchen, clearing the table while he heated the milk, pouring it into the cups and then returning to the fire. With a graceful crossing of her long legs, Katherine sank to the floor with him and placed her cup on the coffee table.

"What about your car?" he asked. "It's still parked in Stillwater."

"That was a rental car. I paid cash and I only owe them for today. I can mail them the money. I have fake identification, so they can't trace it easily. I called the car agency from a pay phone in a restaurant and told them where to find the car."

He nodded. "Where did you meet Sloan?"

"I was a senior in high school. He was a star player on the Louisiana State basketball team and I was dazzled by him when we started dating. We were married a year later, when I was a freshman in college. I'm twenty-three now."

Another surprise, Colin thought, deciding it was the makeup and the severe hairstyle and owlish glasses that made her look older. He started to reach up to remove her glasses, remembered her fear and paused, his hand in the air.

"May I?" he asked and she nodded, looking wary and uncertain. He noticed her quick intake of breath as his fingers brushed her temple and he removed the glasses. He put them on and looked through plain glass.

"I was trying to disguise myself. It's difficult to hide, when you're a five-foot-nine woman."

Colin placed the glasses on the table. "If you married when you were a freshman, you stayed with him a while."

Her face flushed and she rubbed her fingers along the edge of the table. "It's hard to break away, and at first I thought things might change."

"That wasn't any of my business. Sorry."

"I don't mind your asking anything. Sloan was so spectacular, a star athlete, successful, popular, handsome, wealthy, powerful. Too often he made me feel as if I were the one who was at fault or inadequate," she said quietly.

"Do you have any proof of his abuse, if he takes you back to court?"

She shook her head. "No. He bribed and paid off people, and if he didn't his father did."

"There ought to be someone he couldn't get to," Colin said, feeling a growing anger for a man he had never met. "I can check into it if you'd like."

"No!" Her eyes were filled with unmistakable fright. "Please, don't do that. Sloan can be relentless. I don't want anyone hurt because of me and it would just enrage him even more if he learned someone was checking on him."

"I am not afraid of Sloan Manchester," Colin said quietly, not making an effort to hide his anger.

"Please promise me you won't start asking questions in Louisiana."

He knew he was worrying her, so he nodded. "I promise. I not only won't hit you, Katherine, I will never knowingly hurt you."

Her eyes widened with surprise, a feeling that mirrored his own at himself. The words were out without thought and his statement suggested more than he intended. His promise implied a relationship, something he had no intention of developing with her.

"You know what I mean," he said offhandedly, trying to make light of his promise.

She gave him a half smile, her lips curving, a warmth returning to her features, which made his breath catch. His gaze went over her and he forgot about her past and Sloan Manchester. He felt drawn to her, wanting to know her better, wishing he could keep her safe and wondering again at his reaction. What did she really look like without the makeup and with her hair down? His curiosity was rampant as he studied her.

"Can I take down your hair?" he asked, feeling absurd, yet not wanting to frighten her. He suspected the last time he had asked a female a question like that he had been ten years old.

Her eyes seemed to widen as she stared at him and nodded. He reached out carefully with one hand to extract pins, going slowly and trying to avoid even the slightest pull of her hair, as he thought a man could get lost forever in the cool green of her eyes.

As Colin Whitefeather stretched out his hand, Katherine's heart beat with fright and she willed herself to sit still, thinking the first moment he made a move other than to take down her hair, she would put more distance between them. And suppose he wanted her? This afternoon she had placed herself at his mercy and tonight she might have to pay the consequences, because she couldn't run in this storm.

Katherine felt his fingers brush her head, tug so gently on her hair, stirring strange tingles that she was unaccustomed to feeling. Long ago Sloan had killed all physical yearnings toward him. Sex was a dreaded event and she loathed Sloan's touch. Once she started dating Sloan, there had never been another man in her life and she was unaccustomed to anyone wanting to touch her hair.

Her heart thudded with fear and her mouth felt dry while she watched Colin, staring into unfathomable dark eyes that gave no hint as to what he was thinking. His gaze shifted to her hair again as he pulled away another pin and placed it carefully on the table. He was slow and deliberate, barely touching her, not moving an inch closer, and gradually her racing heart slowed to a normal beat.

She began to calm, studying him, realizing his eyes were thickly lashed, his features almost too rugged to be called handsome. His skin was dark, a faint scar visible along his jaw now that she sat close to him and really looked at him.

"Why are you doing this?" she asked quietly.

"I wanted to see what you look like with your hair down." His voice was quiet and deep and reassuring. She couldn't recall a moment like this in her entire marriage to Sloan.

She wished she could make some light comment about her skittishness, yet she couldn't. All afternoon and evening there had been moments when the slightest move on Colin Whitefeather's part would set her heart pounding with apprehension, and it was difficult now to relax. There was no way to forget he was a big, powerful man. And one used to wielding his authority. He threaded his fingers through her hair, combing gently with his big hands. The faint tugs tingled and stirred a strange yearning in her while her gaze locked with his.

Watching her, taking great care, Colin slowly combed free her hair until the mass of it tumbled over her shoulders down to her waist. "Your hair is long," he said in a husky voice, realizing the hints of beauty he had seen earlier were correct. Her hair was a silken cascade that gave her an earthy, touchable look. No practical, sensible hair here, but a mass of vibrant hair that conjured up erotic images of it spilling over her naked body.

"This isn't the real color," she admitted, touching a lock while he continued to comb his fingers through it.

"It's red, isn't it?"

"Yes. I colored it, trying to hide from the men Sloan sent after me. It was useless."

"They're pros and disguises won't do you much good. You're right—you're too tall to really hide from them."

She closed her eyes, feeling as if she had received a blow to her midsection. Was she that obvious?

"Katherine, turn around and I'll give your shoulders a massage that will help you relax," he said gently, trying to get the erotic images out of his mind.

Katherine studied him, gazing into dark eyes that stared back openly, waiting patiently, something she had never known Sloan to do. "Thanks, but that's all right."

"Turn around," he said gently. "You should get used to someone being nice to you."

Colin received another faint half smile as Katherine turned around. Feeling as if he were handling fragile crystal, he reached out carefully and lifted the heavy curtain of hair. She reached up and pulled it all over her right shoulder.

With care he touched her shoulders lightly. She stiffened, drawing a swift breath that he heard and he made his touch even lighter, leaning close to her ear. "I promised you, I won't ever hurt you. Trust me. Pretend it's your friend in California rubbing your shoulders," Colin whispered, damning Sloan Manchester and determined to erase her fear if only for a few minutes.

Katherine shivered, hating his touch, frightened, feeling vulnerable, remembering the early days with Sloan, when he had started out touching her and acting friendly and then suddenly he had been cursing her and hurting her. Remembering too clearly, she gasped and stiffened. His hands stilled instantly.

"Shh, Katherine. It's all right. You're damn tense. I promised I won't hurt you," he whispered as his hands moved again, lightly massaging muscles that she guessed were probably in knots. He rubbed so faintly across her shoulders, keeping his touch impersonal. As he began to massage more strongly, she breathed deeply. Gradually her fear diminished, until finally it was gone. She relaxed, closing her eyes, trusting him and wondering if she would be disappointed.

"I trust you, Colin Whitefeather," she whispered more to herself than him. "Don't betray my trust, because it has been more years than I can remember since I trusted a man."

Colin heard her mumbling and leaned forward and caught the last of her words. His heart lurched and he wanted to cradle her in his arms and tell her she was safe. And he couldn't. If he did, he would be lying through his teeth to her. She would have his protection, probably for less than twenty-four hours. And he couldn't offer her anything more than protection while she was under his roof.

She slanted him a look over her shoulder and his pulse jumped at the curiosity in her green eyes and the faint smile that curved her lips. "You said you're not married. You must date someone."

While they studied each other, he shook his head. Her

eyes were thickly lashed, the dark red lashes curving. For the first time he realized she wasn't wearing mascara on them. She had made her brows thicker, covered her face in thick makeup that was dark beneath her eyes, but her lashes were without the goop she had on her face. He wanted to take his handkerchief and wipe it all away, but he didn't want to alarm her again.

"No. I haven't wanted to date since Dana's death."

"How long ago?"

"Two years, five months and about ten days."

She twisted around to stare at him. With the movement, her hair swirled across her back. "You must have loved her very much," she said with wonder in her voice.

"I did."

"I'm sorry, Colin."

It was the first time she had called him by his first name and a little tingle of awareness startled him.

She turned around to let him continue the massage. He parted her hair, placing half over one shoulder and half over the other—out of the way of his hands. It left a triangle of flesh bare along her nape and he stared at the short locks curling above her collar, the satiny skin that he longed to brush with his fingers. The shorter hair at the nape of her neck was red. As he began to massage, Katherine's shoulders felt delicate, and Colin realized the baggy clothes hid a slender figure because he could feel her shoulder blades through the fuzzy sweater.

"How will you support this baby?"

"I'm studying accounting. I'm taking correspondence courses from Louisiana State. I want to eventually get a degree in accounting."

They sat in silence until finally she turned and scooted away from him, smiling at him. "Thank you. That was relaxing."

She kicked off her shoes and turned to lean back on her

arms and stretch out her long legs, placing her feet in front of the fire. Her tummy looked like a small round ball and he was still amazed she was due in a week.

"You said you've seen doctors. Did they tell you that you'll have a small baby?"

"The last doctor said about six pounds."

"You don't look ready to deliver."

"So how do you know so much about it?" she asked, tilting her head to study him.

"I don't. I've just seen women and worked with women who are pregnant. I've delivered two babies."

"My goodness!" she exclaimed, flashing him a dazzling, dimpled smile that made his heart race. "I'm in good hands then, if this baby decides not to follow the schedule."

"Don't even say it. I was terrified both times. One was a woman caught in a flooded area and another was a woman in a car on the way to the hospital. Somewhere there's a little Colin named after me because of my midwifery."

She laughed, and he wished he could keep her smiling all evening. Sitting on the floor near her feet, he shifted around to face her, locking his arms around his knees with his back to the dying fire. "Feet cold? I can place another log on the fire."

"No need. This is warming my feet."

"What would happen if you called the hometown papers and let them know about the gubernatorial candidate?" he asked. Immediately the shuttered look returned to her eyes.

"I tried that long ago. He's got control of his press. He has good friends there."

"He can't have good friends at every Louisiana paper. Keep trying."

"I won't talk to a reporter about the abuse. I don't have proof and I don't want to bring Sloan's wrath down on me." She shivered. "He would do everything in his power to take my baby from me, because he knows he can get to me that way. I would never see my child again."

Colin's dark eyes narrowed slightly and Katherine felt a chill, aware she was with a man accustomed to fighting for what he thought was right. "You think he might harm his own child?"

"I think Sloan might take my baby, pay someone to raise him or her and keep my child from me. To Sloan, the end justifies the means. He is cruel, ambitious, selfish. He can be a witty, shrewd businessman, a good leader, but he has no heart. His father is the same."

"Would his father condone his taking your baby and hiding him away?"

"His father would probably think they can do much more for a child than I can. Eventually I might find where the child is, but I think all his early years would be gone. I'm not going to try to wreck Sloan's political campaign. I just want to get away and keep my baby with me."

"I don't know you, Katherine, so don't get insulted. Are you certain Sloan is the father?"

Her green eyes focused on him with a flicker of annoyance in them that vanished almost as swiftly as it had come.

"There has never been another man and there never will be again. Sloan *raped* me and I got pregnant right before our divorce."

Colin swore and raked his fingers through his hair, shaking his head. "Sorry for my prying." He studied her as her gaze shifted to the flames and he saw the tiny bits of orange fire reflected in her green irises. He reached over to touch the bottom of her foot slightly and for the first time he had touched her or reached for her, she didn't flinch. He rubbed her foot lightly, feeling the warmth of the bottom of her foot. She wore black cotton socks that disappeared beneath the frayed hems of her jeans. He took her slender foot in his hand to rub it and she laughed softly.

His breath caught because she looked lovely. Her lips curved and even white teeth showed, and her smile radiated warmth. He arched his brows, wishing he could make her laugh more. "What's funny?"

"Do you always give women massages and foot rubs?"

As he slid his fingers over her slender ankle, he shook his head. "Never before that I can recall," he answered. "This is the only way I know that I can touch you without terrifying you."

Her smile vanished. "I don't think I'll ever do well with men again. I can't imagine dating."

He placed her foot on the floor as carefully as if it were fragile china and then he scooted closer to her, watching her eyes widen, but he couldn't detect the fear in them he had seen earlier.

"Does it frighten you for me to sit this close?" he asked quietly.

Her lips firmed as she stared at him. When she shook her head, his heart jumped with satisfaction. He reached out slowly with his finger, taking his time until he touched her cheek and rubbed it lightly. "What's beneath the makeup, Katherine? What are you really like?"

"I'm not sure I know anymore. I'm close to being a basket case, I think. Yet I'm improving, because from the moment I got the divorce I think I began to heal."

"Are you sleepy?" he asked, thinking she should be exhausted after the chase and the cold. If she was truly relaxed, she should be all but falling asleep while he talked. His question brought wariness back to her eyes.

"Maybe a little."

He leaned closer. "Just remember, you're safe. When you get worried, remind yourself you have a cop protecting you and your baby now."

His words erased the wary look and brought a faint smile. "It seems too good to be true."

"It's damn well true," he said gruffly, vowing to himself he would protect her with his life. "Look, you saw my dogs. Anyone I bring on the premises, they know to be a friend." He paused and looked into her green eyes, which watched him attentively. "Actually, I don't bring many people home. But they know you're a friend. They're not friendly to strangers. They're good watchdogs."

"Even in a storm like this?"

"Even in a storm," he reassured her. "In addition to the dogs, I have motion-detector lights and alarms around all the buildings, and there's an alarm at the gate that I can activate if I need to. Most of the time I don't have it on because there are too many living here and going in and out to keep up with it."

"Why are you living in a fortress?"

"I'm a cop. I've made enemies. I'm overly cautious, but I've made some people angry and I don't want to take chances. My folks need me and I intend to stay alive. What I'm leading up to—you're in a safer place than you have been. Those guys can track me down, because my blue pickup stands out like an orange-haired whore in church. Even if it had been black and like a hundred others, they had chances to get my tag number. They may try to come out here after you."

"I didn't mean to bring trouble to you."

"I'm the one who said get into the car. If I'm out feeding stock or anything else and those guys show up, you call 911. You tell them we have a prowler. No one will ask you questions about your past. They'll think I've brought home a girlfriend."

"I thought you didn't date."

"I don't, but everyone expects me to start dating. Will you dial 911?"

"Yes."

"Good. And as soon as you hang up, go to the bunk-house. If there's anyone there, tell him to get me. Do you know how to use a gun?"

"I bought one and went to the range to practice about three times."

"You're carrying it now. Get it out if you hear someone when you're here alone. Just don't shoot me."

"I don't really think I can shoot anyone."

"They won't know that. A gun stops people from doing all sorts of things. Those thugs may trace you to me, but they won't take you here. As soon as they realize the risks they run out here, they'll back off to wait and get you somewhere else. They'll know you won't stay with me indefinitely."

She blinked as if she were thinking about what he told her, and then she nodded. "So I'm safe here?"

"Yes, you're safe," he said, knowing no one could be one-hundred-percent sure of anything in this world but that she needed some reassurance. He couldn't promise her as much when the storm abated and he drove her to Tulsa to the airport.

The phone rang, cutting into the quiet. Colin stood, crossing the room to a table to pick up the receiver. She turned to look at the fire, watching the orange flames and the glowing embers in the logs, which were turning to ash. She heard him replace the receiver and turned around to find him studying her.

"That was the sheriff's department. Some men have been asking around town about me."

Four

He went to the window to gaze outside and then returned to sit down near her. "A friend in the department let me know. They don't take kindly to strangers asking questions about where one of their own lives."

"It had to be the men after me."

"Stillwater is still a small enough town that word got back to the department about two strangers asking questions. People told them I live on a ranch."

Her wide-eyed gaze shifted to the windows and Colin knew her worries were returning.

"Katherine," he said gently, "I'm going to protect you. I told you that I have lights, alarms, fences and dogs. You have me, and I have guns and am trained in fighting. Right now we're in a raging blizzard and they're not going to come in this storm. It's too hazardous for them. Relax while you're here."

Reassured, Katherine partially agreed with him. Yet her

nerves were stretched thin. "The night Sloan raped me, I had already gotten an apartment in New Orleans and moved away from him. I thought I had total security in my apartment. He talked the landlord out of the key. Sloan surprised me in the night. I woke up and he was in my room."

"Afterward, did you call a crisis center—talk to anyone about what he did?" Colin wished he could have five minutes alone with Sloan Manchester.

"I ended up in the emergency room at the hospital. He had broken my collarbone. My injury was wiped off the records."

"It has to be on a record somewhere, if you know the right people. If you'd give me any dates—"

"No! I'm not going to fight him. I'm not going back."

"Calm down. Even if you don't fight him or go back willingly, you should give me dates and names. I can do more to find records than you can because of my connections. If those goons get you, wouldn't you like someone to try to fight for you?"

Her eyes widened and she stared at him with such intensity that he wondered if anyone in her life had ever before offered to help her. Her eyes were crystal, a deep, clear green that was fascinating. Fringed with thick lashes, her big eyes held him spellbound. He wanted to touch her lightly, but he kept his hands to himself. "Lady, you've had to fight too many of your own battles," he said softly. "Give me some ammunition so I can help if you need it."

Licking her lips, she shook her head. He watched the tip of her tongue slide sensuously across her full lower lip and then trace her upper lip. His body tightened and an uncustomary yearning struck him forcefully. He wanted to place his mouth over hers, to feel those wet, soft lips beneath his.

Tearing his thoughts from that speculation, he looked into her eyes again.

"Do you always rush to the aid of strangers?" she asked.

"That's part of being a cop. Sometimes you help strangers."

"I haven't found any other cops offering help."

"I doubt if you've given any a chance."

"I don't want to pull you into my problems."

"Someday you may need a friend. You don't want to lose this baby to Sloan. Give me some dates and names, and then if anything ever happens to you and you want me to try to get facts about your injuries I'll have a place to start. All you'd have to do is get word to me that you need help."

He wondered if she had completely driven all sense from his head. Why was he arguing with the woman? Usually when he helped strangers, it was a situation that was thrust upon him. He didn't usually ask to walk into a nest of snakes. And tangling with Sloan Manchester's power would be far more dangerous than a nest of snakes.

"Even if I wanted your help, I don't want to turn his anger on you," she said solemnly, her green eyes holding a look of fear that made Colin's temperature rise a notch. "I think when Sloan was in college he hurt a man very badly and his father covered it up. I think they paid the man's family a small fortune to keep them from going to the police. Sloan has a violent temper that he keeps hidden from the public. And he can be very charming when he wants."

"Obviously," Colin remarked dryly, "or he wouldn't have lasted this long." Colin made a mental note to try to find out about the man Sloan had hurt so badly.

"He works out, too. He thinks his body is beautiful. He

builds muscle and he likes to look at himself. He's taken karate and he's incredibly strong."

"I'm not afraid of Sloan Manchester. And I've had a lot of practice in taking care of myself. Give me some dates and names." Colin waited, both of them staring at each other.

"I'll have to try to remember," she said finally in a quiet voice. "I don't know that I can recall accurately. It isn't something I've tried to remember."

He stood. "I'll get a tablet to write down what you tell me."

Katherine hugged her knees as she watched Colin cross the room to a desk and rummage in a drawer. His jeans molded his trim buttocks and long legs. When he turned around, he had a tablet in his hands and he thumbed through the pages. While his attention was elsewhere, her gaze ran over him again.

The tight, worn jeans cupped and emphasized his masculinity. His hips were slender and the jeans rode low on them. She marveled that he was going to help her. And down deep, she still could not let go of her fear and really trust him. He was too big, too strong, too male for her to assume he was just what he said.

Colin Whitefeather seemed interested in her welfare. But for the first six months of her marriage, Sloan had been the same way. And Katherine couldn't change her attitude toward men like switching on a light. She didn't know whether she could ever change it again.

Dinner, the warmth of the fire, the semblance of safety, all had caused her to relax for the first time in too long to remember, and in spite of her wariness, exhaustion enveloped her. It was an effort to avoid curling up on the rug and going to sleep.

"Other than to eat, do your dogs ever come into the house?" she asked.

"Sure. But they have a dog door in the garage and when I need them to watch the grounds I leave them out. They like this kind of weather. Especially Lobo. Heaven knows what his ancestors thrived on. There's a wild streak in his blood."

"There must be one in yours, too," she said quietly, and Colin's brows arched.

"I haven't done anything wild tonight."

"You did today when you opened your car door and told me to get in. You're an ex-cop. You have a wild side."

He sat down by her and she felt a tremor, wanting to scoot away, yet sitting still. Maybe he was really what he said. Maybe she could really trust him. Maybe.

"Hear me out before you protest," he said carefully. "I can call a reporter and just tell him to look into Sloan's past. The reporter wouldn't have to have any more information than that. Not my name or your name. You'd be out of it. Reporters can smell a story like a dog can smell meat."

She shook her head. "Sloan would have the story killed and the reporter fired."

"Maybe in his hometown, but Sloan is running for governor. If I call a reporter in a different city—"

"No!" she exclaimed, and Colin was startled by the vehemence in her reply. "Promise me you won't. Please."

He didn't have to promise her anything—and it would be in her best interests if he called a reporter—but as he gazed into her wide eyes there was only one thing he could do. He nodded his head.

"All right, but I think you're wrong."

"Say it. Say you promise you won't tip off a reporter."

"I promise I will not call a reporter about your ex without your permission."

"Thank you," she said, her lashes lowering. "I just

want to get away from Sloan and protect my baby from him.''

Colin handed her two calendars. "Here's this year and last. Can you give me any date? Start with the last time he hurt you."

She flipped pages, turning back through the previous year's calendar. "May thirteenth last year. I went to Memorial Hospital emergency. I was admitted as Katherine Benedette, my maiden name." She watched as he bent over the tablet and wrote in a bold scrawl. The pen paused.

"Do you remember a doctor?"

"Buford White is an old family friend of Sloan's father."

Colin raised his head. "Give me another name. You didn't just see one doctor. What time were you admitted?"

"I can't remember."

"Come on, make a guess. Early evening? Midnight?"

"It was well after midnight. I would guess about two in the morning."

"Do you have any other name? A nurse? An intern?"

"There was a nurse named Debbie. I don't know her last name. She's short, blond, blue eyes. I've seen her before and she's very kind."

"Good. Where did you and Sloan live?"

"Baton Rouge. But he has friends all over Louisiana, particularly New Orleans. He's president of Manchester Enterprises now. His father is CEO."

Colin glanced at her and then raised his head to study her closer. "Are you tired?"

She nodded. "It's the first time I've relaxed in a long time, and today was particularly bad."

"You should have told me. C'mon. I'll get my things out of my room."

"Please let me just sleep on your sofa. I don't want to put you out of your bed," her words tumbled out too fast.

She knew she should trust him and forget her fears, but the suggestion to go into his bedroom worried her.

Colin listened to the rush of words and saw the fear back in her eyes. He wanted to put his arm around her shoulders and reassure her and lead her to his bedroom, but he knew better. "I'll go get my things, and then you take my room. I won't argue about that. I can keep a better watch on the place out here."

"Oh!" Her mouth was open while she glanced toward the windows, and again he felt an urge to place his lips against hers. Unable to understand the reaction he was having to her, he clamped his jaw closed and strode to his room. As he pulled jeans from the closet, he heard a knock and turned. She stood in the open doorway. She looked frightened, and he wondered how he could reassure her further that she needn't be afraid.

"Don't hurry. And don't change the sheets. I don't mind. I've slept all sorts of places."

He nodded, picking up a pair of topsiders. "You know where the bathroom and towels are. Want anything, just holler."

He carried his things toward the door. She scooted out of his way, and he passed her without a glance. As he crossed the room, he tossed one of his clean chambray shirts onto the bed.

"Here's a shirt you can sleep in, if you'd like."

"Colin." The word was tentative and soft-spoken.

"Yes," he replied, curious about what she wanted. She stood behind a rocker, as if trying to keep a barrier between them.

"Thank you."

"You're welcome. Get some sleep." He left and closed the door behind him, letting out his breath. He felt as if he had been handling something incredibly fragile all evening long. He dropped his things on a chair and hit the light switch. Moving to the windows, he opened the shutters slightly to see outside. A world of white was all that was visible. No one could be dumb enough to come out in this, and if they did they would be stuck long before they reached his place. Tonight would be a peaceful night's sleep.

He pulled off his red shirt, got a blanket from the closet and stretched out on the sofa, placing his pistol on the table beside him. Thoughts and images of Katherine swirled in his mind like snowflakes drifting against the window. Sloan Manchester. The bastard. One call to the right reporter could stir an investigation that would uncover Sloan's past. Now Colin knew, after his promise to Katherine, he could never make that call.

But once she was on a plane to California he could do his own investigating. He could find evidence and people. No one could pay off the world. There would be people in the hospital, people who knew Katherine, who would come forth for her. If he could just find witnesses, it would take so little to bare Manchester's evil to the world. Not everyone would fear Sloan Manchester. A man with the arrogance of Manchester would leave a trail of enemies in his wake. Colin shifted restlessly. Before the trail got any colder he intended to try to locate some witnesses for Katherine.

Swearing, he sat up in the darkness and glanced toward his closed bedroom door. Why in the sweet hell was he getting so involved in this woman's life? He didn't need to stick his neck out and go after Sloan Manchester. He didn't need to try to find evidence of Katherine's abuse.

He lay back down, knowing that as soon as he put her on a plane to California, he would head for Louisiana. No one with a past like Manchester's deserved to win an election. In the meantime, he had to protect Katherine from the goons while running his ranch. When the snow stopped flying, they'd be after her again.

Katherine woke and stretched, for an instant feeling content and safe. The sensation was so unusual that she blinked and looked around the masculine bedroom, with its clutter and fishing gear and guns. Memories of Colin Whitefeather rushed back, reminding her why she felt safe. And with surprise, she realized she had slept soundly all through the night.

She felt the baby move and placed her hand protectively on her stomach. "It's getting close to the time for you to come into the world," she said softly and smiled.

Turning her head, she glanced at the floor-to-ceiling glass doors and the panoramic view of snow-covered land beyond them. Her smile vanished as she shoved back covers and climbed out of bed. Her body felt heavy and cumbersome and she had a slight nagging ache in the center of her back. She rubbed at it, thinking about California and Paula waiting. "Soon we'll be where it's warm and sunny, just in time for your grand entrance," she said, rubbing her tummy again. "So soon. Just wait until next week and by then you'll have a nursery ready and a crib and little gowns. All right? And I have to get you a name. Emily? Jacob? Cade?"

She crossed the room to gaze outside. Snow sparkled in the sunlight and the sky was a deep, clear blue. The storm had ended and the men could come after her. Feeling a sudden sense of panic, she glanced down.

Colin's blue shirt hung to her knees. She had turned back the sleeves. It was worn; the elbows had only a few threads and the garment seemed to carry an aura of his presence. She was in his room, in his bed during the night, in his shirt now.

And she had been undisturbed all night. So he could be

trusted. Yet every time she almost had herself convinced, she remembered when she had trusted Sloan and how he had smashed that trust completely. As she smoothed covers on the bed, she glanced at the clock and paused in surprise. It was nine o'clock in the morning!

She showered and washed her hair, watching the brown rinse swirl in the water and disappear down the drain. For today she wouldn't try to hide her hair. Blow-drying her hair, she let it fall straight, combing the long strands that reached her waist.

She dressed in the baggy jeans that gave room for her swollen tummy, then she pulled on her fuzzy purple sweater, which hung to mid-thigh. Slipping on a headband to hold her hair back from her face, she went to find Colin.

The kitchen held delightful aromas, the rich brew of coffee and the sweet tang of cinnamon. A note was propped up in the middle of the oak table. She looked at the scrawl that was becoming familiar.

"At work. Back by noon. Alarm on. Breakfast fixings in kit. Snow too deep for them to get through."

She laughed at the brief sentences. The man did not believe in flowery speech. She reread the note, looking at the last statement. She dropped the note onto the table and went to the front to look at the drive.

She couldn't find it for the undisturbed sparkling blanket of snow that spread endlessly. Reassured, she turned to look at the empty room. She began a second tour of the house, this time at a leisurely pace, looking in drawers, curious about Colin and what kind of man he was.

She discovered he read books about true crime. He had fishing rods and guns. And on a shelf in his closet she found a few rodeo trophies for calf roping. Pulling open a wide dresser drawer, she found a picture of him with a woman who must have been his wife. She looked at the slender, smiling blonde. They had their arms around each other. The blonde was looking into the camera while Colin was looking at her.

Sympathy stirred for his loss, and Katherine replaced the picture. His underwear and socks were stuffed into the drawer in a jumble with belt buckles, a coil of rope and boxes of ammunition. He did not spend too much time tidying up, although the house seemed clean. She closed the drawer and a white triangle of cotton briefs stuck out. She opened the drawer and tucked the briefs inside, momentarily thinking about him wearing them. His tight jeans had molded his body and she could imagine what he would look like in the briefs—the image sent a warm tingle spiraling down in her. The reaction shocked her. She didn't think she could have a strong, positive physical reaction to a man again. And to have it while she was pregnant was even more surprising. For so long she had felt numb around men in general. Repulsed and frightened by Sloan.

She stopped prying into Colin's life and returned to the kitchen to get breakfast. Looking out the window to the west, she saw the other ranch buildings, which had been hidden in the blinding storm the previous night. The barn was large and looked as if it had been built in recent years. Three horses milled in an adjoining corral. Beyond the barn was a long, low building that she guessed was the bunkhouse. To the east of the bunkhouse were other outbuildings, a toolshed and metal buildings. As she poured fresh orange juice and swallowed her vitamins, the phone rang.

Without thinking, she picked it up. "Whitefeather's," she answered. The moment she spoke, she wished she had let the phone ring and never touched it.

There was silence and then a click.

Turning to ice, she stared at the receiver and then slammed it down. Why had she answered? For months she had been overly cautious. What kind of spell had Colin

Whitefeather woven, that she had relaxed enough to let
down her guard?

"Damn," she swore, closing her eyes and clinging to
the counter. "Don't answer the phone! Don't answer the
phone!" she repeated to herself, but she knew it was too
late. If they had called to see if she was at his house, she
had just given them their answer.

She rushed to the front again, for a moment wanting to
flee on foot she was so frightened. Reason asserted itself
and she calmed, staring at the deep snow. In the distance
was a solitary oak, its trunk covered with snow and blend-
ing into the surroundings, but some of the brown branches
were dark against the morning sky. She would see anyone
approaching the house. Colin had a clear view in all di-
rections for miles, except to the west of the house where
the barn and bunk and outbuildings were.

Wondering how soon she could get to Tulsa and a plane
west, she looked at the snowdrifts blown up against the
barn. She couldn't imagine getting through today and
thinking about leaving stirred opposing emotions. She worried about every delay. It was time for the baby's arrival
and she wanted—and had planned—to be in California by
now.

At the same time, she felt safe here and she dreaded
leaving. That notion surprised her. In his quiet way, Colin
Whitefeather had torn down more barriers than she had
realized.

Noticing that what had been a clear sky was now dotted
with clouds, she called the airlines. She asked about flights
to San Francisco, but she didn't make reservations. As she
replaced the receiver, a motor rumbled, drawing closer to
the house. Her pulse jumped with alarm and she rushed to
the window. One glance outside and she let out her breath
with relief as she recognized Colin's broad-brimmed black
hat and broad shoulders. He drove a tractor to the back

door and climbed out of the enclosed cab. The dogs came bounding after him.

Suddenly self-conscious, she shook her head, her fall of hair swinging behind her shoulders. Feeling awkward and unattractive, she was aware of her baggy pants and her pregnant condition.

When Colin opened the door, the dogs rushed in past him. "Katherine!" he bellowed and then saw her standing across the room. As he looked at her, his heart thudded against his rib cage. The thick makeup, as well as the penciled-in heavy brows, the shadows beneath her eyes and the mousy brown hair were gone.

She was stunning with a cascade of shimmering red hair, flawless skin, rosy cheeks. The bulky sweater that hung to her knees almost hid her condition, and for an instant he mentally imagined how she might look when she was not pregnant. And when she was naked.

"Good morning," she said shyly, smiling at him, and something inside him seemed to unlock and open.

He tossed his hat on a hook and shrugged out of his coat while the dogs milled around her and she petted them. "Good morning," he replied and turned to look at her again. He crossed the room without taking his gaze from her.

As he approached her, all color drained from her face and she backed up a step. "What's wrong?"

Puzzled, he frowned, and she backed up another step, glancing toward the door as if she might bolt down the hall. "Damn," he groaned and stopped in his tracks, holding his hands out. "Am I frightening you?"

She fidgeted with the collar of her sweater nervously, but the color rushed back into her cheeks. She shook her head, causing the fall of hair to ripple, making him want to wind his hands in it. "No, you were just staring so intently. Colin, I can't react in normal ways."

"The hell you can't," he said gently. "First, always remind yourself that I promised I would never knowingly hurt you. Second, when you're in my house, relax."

He received another dimpled smile that warmed him more than the cozy kitchen. He moved closer to her, walking slowly to make certain he didn't see alarm jump back into her eyes. "I was staring for a reason."

"What reason?" she asked, and he had to bite back a smile because she sounded genuinely puzzled.

"The makeup you wore yesterday is gone and your hair is its natural color."

"Oh, yes. I didn't put it up—" she said, picking up long strands.

"Don't put it up," he said in a husky voice. He took the locks from her fingers to let them slide over his. "I was staring because you're a pretty woman."

A flush turned her face rosy as her eyes widened with surprise. "I can't be." She gave him a slight smile. "I'm nine months pregnant, Colin. Not to mention being taller than many men. But thank you."

He couldn't resist. He caught more of her hair and ran it across his cheek, wanting to feel its cool, silky touch, wanting to touch her and knowing he would have to be so very careful if he did. He longed to caress the hair, to draw her closer and kiss her.

"You're beautiful when you're nine months pregnant," he said quietly. "And you're not taller than I am."

Her big green eyes studied him as if she still doubted he could possibly find her attractive. And then her lips parted and her gaze went over his features. As if realizing how blatantly she was studying him, she blushed and turned her head, long hair hiding her features. "Thank you. I can't remember ever being called beautiful."

He wanted to turn her around and kiss her. Clamping his jaw shut and jamming his hands in his pockets, he moved abruptly away from her and accidentally stepped on Buster's tail. The dog yelped and jumped and Colin swore, bending down to pet the dog.

"Sorry, boy, didn't see you."

The dog wagged his tail and Colin moved to the sink to get a drink of water.

"I called the airlines, but I haven't made a reservation," she said. "I didn't know whether I could get out of here today or not."

"I'm going to clear the ranch road. I've already checked with the highway patrol. The county road isn't open yet." He turned to cross his legs at the ankles and lean against the counter. "I think I can get you to Tulsa tomorrow, if you want to make reservations."

She nodded.

"You may have that baby on the plane."

Smiling, she shook her head. "No, it's not due tomorrow."

"Yeah, I know. You have another six whole days," he said dryly. "I hope that baby understands the schedule."

"I hope so, too."

He glanced over his shoulder through the window at the sky, which was becoming more overcast.

"Colin," she said hesitantly, and he shot her a glance, the hairs on his neck prickling at her tone. Something was wrong. Something had happened. He could hear it in her voice. And at the same time, on another level, he was too conscious of the sound of his name when she said it. The woman had climbed into his car and into his life with surprising swiftness. Maybe next time he thought about rescuing someone, he would remember to mind his own business.

"I was getting my breakfast and the phone rang."

"You answered." He gave a moment's thought to the men coming after her. He and his men were armed, warned and ready. The roads weren't good. If the guys after her were stupid enough to make a try on his place, they must not have asked too many questions in town. He wondered if they knew she was staying with an ex-cop.

"I'm sorry. I just didn't think. I haven't been around a phone in a long time."

"It's done. It won't change anything."

"No one spoke. There was just silence and then a click."

"Ninety-nine chances out of one hundred it was them. So now we can figure that they know for certain you're still here. Don't worry about it. Let me do the worrying, and while you're here I'll keep you safe. Everyone who works for me is packing a weapon today. I've got a small army out there and the sheriff's department is just a call away."

"I don't want to talk to the sheriff!"

"You won't have to. If I call him for help, I don't have to explain any reason the men were trying to get in here. Total strangers. We don't know anything about them."

"If the police come, I'll have to give them my name."

"So give it. I didn't recognize it. Even if they do, you said your ex-husband hadn't made it public that he's searching for you." As she nodded, he set down his glass. "I'm going to clear the drive."

She followed him to the door and he paused. "If you want to go out in the snow, I can give you some other clothes when you come in. Look in my closet and get a pair of my boots to wear. Take anything you want."

"Thanks."

He couldn't resist. He bent and brushed a light kiss across her soft cheek. He paused, saw her eyes held a questioning look but no fear. Whistling for the dogs, he jammed his hat on his head and went outside.

She touched her cheek, staring at the tall man striding

toward the tractor. He thought she looked beautiful! Nine months pregnant and for the past month she had felt awkward and unattractive. With Colin Whitefeather, he not only made her feel attractive and like a woman again, he made her feel dainty and small. It was a novel feeling and one she liked. She touched her cheek where he had brushed such a slight kiss, yet it had warmed her more than a roaring fire could have.

"You're a good man, Colin Whitefeather," she said quietly, watching him bouncing in the cab of the tractor.

He turned, the tractor pushing the snow away while the dogs bounded in the snow. Suddenly she wanted to go out. It had been too long to remember since she had done anything really frivolous. She closed the door and rushed to his closet, pulling on the most worn pair of boots she could find, gathering up her coat and returning to his dresser to unerringly get a pair of leather gloves she remembered seeing when she was snooping in his things earlier.

By the time she went outside, he already had cleared a long swath and was down the road. The dogs spotted her and came running back, racing around her while she made prints in the snow, laughing for no reason, feeling secure for the first time in years. She rolled snow into a ball and then began in earnest to build a snowman.

She worked, finally looking at the tall snowman. She went to the kitchen to get a carrot for a nose and two small tomatoes for eyes. She found a battered cotton cap and placed it on the snowman's head, standing back to look at her handiwork.

When she began to feel the cold, she went inside and pulled off Colin's boots. She shed her baggy jeans, throwing them in the washer with some of her things. The sweater came to midthigh and she didn't expect him back until supper. She found a pair of his woolen socks and pulled them on, going to see what supplies he had and what she might cook for dinner.

And she made plane reservations in Tulsa for a flight tomorrow to San Francisco, leaving Oklahoma at three in the afternoon. As she replaced the receiver, she looked at Colin's kitchen. She would never forget the tall cop. He was a rancher now but she could see him only as a cop, in spite of this land that was his home and livelihood.

He came in after dark, calling her name before he opened the door. She turned from the stove and Colin yanked off his jacket while the dogs ran past him to her.

"Something smells great!"

She shrugged. "I may be rusty. I haven't really cooked in a long time. I found salmon fillets in the freezer and thawed them."

He crossed the kitchen in long strides and raised the lid on a pan. Steam rose when he looked at golden rice.

"I made my plane reservations for tomorrow afternoon."

He closed the pan and nodded. "I'll get you to Tulsa if I can, but we're supposed to have another storm blow in here and it's already snowing now."

"No!" She crossed to the windows, rubbing a frosted pane and staring outside. "No!"

"Don't panic. If you have to stay here and go to the Stillwater or Tulsa hospital, I'll stay with you."

She turned around. "Why are you doing so much for me?" She rubbed her forehead. "Sorry, Colin. I should just say thank you and not ask."

"You can ask anything you want," he said. "I'm offering help because I think you need it." Then he grinned with a flash of white teeth that made her feel weak-kneed. "Let's face it, lady," he drawled, crossing the room to her, stopping short of touching her, "you're a beautiful

woman and I'm dazzled. Your looks will get you all kinds
of offers and help.''

Laughing, she blushed. "Thank you, I think. It's a little
difficult to believe that line, Colin, when I'm shaped like
a barrel!" She looked outside again and her smile vanished. "If we get more snow, I don't know what I'll do. I
have to get to California."

A loud buzz began to sound repeatedly. "That's the
alarm at the front gate," he said tersely, drawing a gun
from his belt.

Five

Colin yanked up the phone as he held his pistol. "Lock yourself in my bedroom and stay away from the windows and doors—" He turned back to the phone. "Abe, I need help. The alarm's going. Men trying to get in here. There may be shooting."

He slammed down the phone and punched another number. "Bud, the alarm's sounding. Stay where you are. I can hold them off here and I've called the sheriff."

Frightened, she stood rooted to the spot as she listened to him. He hung up the receiver, yanked on his jacket and ran out of the room. She followed, her heart racing while she watched him remove a rifle from his gun case and then run back to the kitchen. "Lock the door behind me," he yelled.

"Where are you going?" she asked, horrified that he might be driving out to look for the men.

"Up on the roof." Colin slammed the door and Katherine locked it quickly. She switched off all the lights in the house and went to the front. Tiny flakes of snow fell and she studied the gray sky. She laced her fingers together nervously, terrified Colin would get hurt fighting for her.

She glanced at the road Colin had cleared. How long would it take the new snow to obliterate it? Would the sheriff be able to get here in time to help? She heard a bump and went back to the kitchen. A ladder was propped against the back of the house. Something scraped overhead and she guessed Colin was on the roof. She walked to the front room to watch, guessing they would come from that direction.

Within minutes a car appeared on the road, a dark shape against the white. She stared at it, amazed that they would boldly drive up to his house. When she had heard the alarm sound, she supposed Sloan's men were on the grounds and would try to slip up to the house undetected. It hadn't occurred to her they would drive right up to the front door.

She started to the kitchen to open the door because she guessed Colin would come inside when he saw them. Before she had taken more than a step from the window, the blast of Colin's rifle shattered the quiet. The gunshot made her jump, even though the sound was muffled since she was inside and it was out.

Another shot rang out, and then a volley of shots. A window shattered and she stepped back, her heart pounding. She looked out again and the car had turned and was heading back up the road toward the highway. Leaning against the wall with relief, she remembered Colin might be locked out. She hurried to the kitchen, and when she opened the door he stepped inside.

"I think the bastards are gone. I'm going up to the gate and check the alarm. By that time, the sheriff will arrive. I may bring him back here with me."

"All right," she said, locking the door behind Colin,

wondering why she felt so completely safe with him. She would prefer to avoid the sheriff, yet with Colin beside her she suspected the sheriff would accept her and not ask questions. In minutes she saw Colin drive past in his Jeep.

As soon as he was out of sight she covered the front window with cardboard she found in the pantry, and then she sat watching for his return. Snowflakes swirled, becoming larger and she stared at them, thinking about her plane reservation. It was half an hour before Colin reappeared, without the sheriff. "Abe went on back to town."

"Does he know about me?"

"He knows I have a woman up here. I told him you have a jealous ex-husband. That should start all kinds of gossip about me in town."

"I didn't mean to bring trouble," she said perfunctorily, looking at him holding his rifle. He looked formidable and tough, and her mistrust rose like a specter.

"Lady, I knew I was courting trouble when I told you to hop into my pickup," he remarked dryly, giving her a faint smile and then pausing to tilt his head and study her. "What's wrong?" he asked quietly.

"You look so tough," she said in a small voice. "The rifle..."

"Isn't aimed at you. It's in my hand for your protection. Just keep that in mind," he said solemnly and left the kitchen. She followed him, standing in the doorway while he placed the gun in the rack. "I'll reset the alarm, but they drove through the gate and broke the lock."

"How are the roads?"

"Bad. Abe came in a Jeep and he has chains. I have chains, but we had so much ice that the chains don't do as much good as on snow," he said while he returned to the kitchen to hang up his coat and hat.

"I need to get out of here tomorrow."

He turned to her, placing his hands lightly on her shoulders. Colin gazed down at her, conscious that she didn't flinch this time when he reached for her. "We'll try to get out in the morning. Tonight, forget about those goons. They won't be back."

"How can you be sure?"

"They found out today that they're not just chasing a pregnant woman. This is too tough a place. I can see them coming. I have dogs and an alarm. They're going to get shot at, and if they get caught between me and the sheriff, they'll be in deep trouble. Your ex probably has instructed them to avoid getting picked up by the law and raising questions."

"I'm sure he has!"

"Okay. They'll stay on the highway somewhere and watch for you to leave. Or they'll just head for the airports to wait for you. You've thrown them a curve by finding someone who'll shoot back."

"I hope you're right. None of your men saw them coming."

"Unless some of the men are working up by the gate and road, they won't see anyone."

"Your front window is broken. I put cardboard over it."

"We've got glass in the barn. I'll cut a piece and replace it when the storm stops. I've had to replace broken windows before—although not from gunshots."

She motioned toward the stove. "If you're about ready to eat, I'll put the fish on now."

"Nope." He crossed the room to switch on the alarm and to get dog food. "As soon as I feed the hungry horde, I'll do the cooking. You sit down and watch and talk to me."

"I can get dinner while you feed the dogs."

"You don't have to. Sit down," he said as he opened the door to the garage and both dogs bounded inside, running to her.

Sitting, she petted them, feeling the thick fur on both animals. Colin hoisted a huge sack of dog food to his shoulder, and the dogs left her to follow him into the garage while she washed up and continued getting dinner.

In minutes he was back to lead her to a chair before washing his hands. He put the fish under the broiler and placed rolls in the oven.

"Looks good to me," he said.

She watched him work and wondered about him. "Tell me about growing up. I don't know anything about you."

"It's simple. I was born in Oklahoma, I played football, went to Missouri University on a scholarship and got a degree in criminal justice. I joined a county sheriff's department in Missouri, did undercover work. Dad has always farmed, but they did live near Anadarko, Oklahoma."

She stood to help pour water and he caught her wrist. She gasped and jerked her arm free.

"Katherine," he said.

Instantly she regretted her action and was embarrassed by it. "I'm sorry, Colin. I'm not accustomed to a man grabbing my wrist and having it mean anything except he's going to hold me while he hits me."

Colin ached to pull her into his arms and reassure her and stroke away every terrible memory from her mind, but he knew that was impossible. "Some day," he said in a husky voice, "I'll reach for you like that without thinking and you won't jump away. You'll get over him."

"I gave you the date I was last with him. Do you know how many months ago that was? Soon it'll have been a year, yet I still jump at every move you make. I'll never be normal again," she said, looking at the window and watching snow swirling against the pane.

"Yes, you will," Colin rejoined firmly. "Now, sit down and relax and let me cook for you."

"I can do a few things."

"When you get to California, you'll be doing everything for two. Let me do this."

Nodding, she sat and watched him, still embarrassed by her reaction, wondering about his patience. At what point would he be pushed over an edge? Sloan said everyone had one, that point where they could no longer tolerate a situation.

Finally dinner was on the table. The pink salmon was lightly covered in a lemon-dill sauce, and Colin sighed. "This is great! Beats my dinners to pieces."

"Thank you. It's pretty simple."

They ate in a comfortable silence, but curiosity about him continued to nag her. "How long were you married?"

As his dark eyes met hers, she could see the warmth fade from his expression.

"Sorry, Colin. I didn't mean to pry."

"I told you, ask whatever you want. We were married five years. We wanted a baby, but Dana hadn't gotten pregnant."

Colin wondered if it would ever get less painful to talk about. Memories always hurt. And he knew without Katherine asking, that she was wondering what had happened. Anyone would and tonight when he had gone to his room and opened his drawer, he realized she had been in his things. She had probably seen Dana's picture. And she had a healthy curiosity.

"Dana was killed by a bomb meant for me," he said stiffly.

"Oh, my heavens! Colin, I'm sorry. You don't have to tell me," Katherine said, shocked by his answer.

"It's all right," he replied gruffly. "I helped catch the men that did it and put them away, and then I resigned. There was a time I was threatened, and I moved my folks to their place and then when I quit, I moved here."

His gaze shifted to her and he saw she was no longer eating. He glanced at her plate. "Go ahead and finish your dinner."

She had lost all appetite. The pain showed in the lines around his mouth and the cold, flat look in his eyes. And she realized this incredibly rugged man, who seemed stronger and tougher than Sloan ever had, was vulnerable where his heart was concerned.

Without thinking, she reached across the table and placed the palm of her hand against his cheek. "I'm sorry that she's gone," Katherine said.

His gaze met hers and his pained look vanished. He arched his brow and placed his hand over hers, giving her a questioning look.

"You're not scared of me any longer?" he asked softly.

Her pulse jumped. How had the moment changed so swiftly? The look in his eyes now was totally focused on her. "All I can say is that I'm not afraid of you this moment," she replied, wondering whether that was the absolute truth or not.

"That's very good, Katherine," he said. Holding her hand, he turned his head slightly to brush a kiss across her fingers. His breath was warm, his lips made featherlight touches that started tingles in her. "I'll be praying for you and that little baby of yours when you're in California."

She was touched because she had glimpsed the wounds and the goodness in the tough warrior. "I'm glad you opened the pickup door."

He winked at her. "Can you eat a little more?"

She looked down at cold food. "I'm not hungry now."

"Neither am I. I'll clean—"

"No! I can help clean. You worked outside all day and fought off those men. I'd think that would exhaust you."

"I'd like to get my hands on them."

She turned to look at him. "I hope with all my heart

that you don't. I'll be in California this time tomorrow night. Once I'm gone, you'll never see them again."

Colin carried dishes to the sink and felt a little lurch at the thought of her leaving, and then realized how ridiculous that was. She was no part of his life and he had spent only a brief amount of time with her—just a little over twenty-four hours, yet it seemed as if he had known her for a long time.

He paused to watch her clearing the table. She fit into his life as if she had always been in it. The idea surprised him and he studied her, watching the shimmering curtain of hair as she leaned forward. He found her sexy and he wondered at himself. He hadn't felt that way about any woman since he lost Dana. Now here was a woman nine months pregnant, dressed in baggy clothes that hid every curve, and he wanted her.

He inhaled deeply, turning to work as if demons were after him, struggling to get his body under control. As he banged shut the dishwasher door, she looked at him and laughed. "If you've worked that fast and furiously all day, I'd think you would be exhausted now. Maybe there's a competitive side to you—trying to outclean me here?"

He moved over to put his hands on either side of her, gripping the counter and hemming her in. Last night she would have panicked, but now she gazed up at him with curiosity.

"No, I'm not a damned bit competitive about cleaning a kitchen. I was just trying to get my thoughts off the very attractive woman who is with me."

"That's nice, but so foolish, Colin. I feel like a blimp," she added, her eyes going wide while her cheeks turned pink. "You need to get out and date," she said, bumping his arm.

Instantly he moved away and inhaled deeply again, trying to resist the urge to pull her into his arms and show her just exactly how attractive she was to him. "Let's build a fire in the front room."

As soon as he had made a roaring fire, they sat on the floor near it while sleet pelted the window. "What will I do if I'm snowed in here again tomorrow?"

"Change your reservation to the next day. Or stay with me, and I'll get you to the Stillwater or Tulsa hospital."

"I can't remain here. Those men are too close. You've already been too involved and put in too much danger. And I don't want to go to a hospital where they can find us."

Colin touched her chin and tilted her head up so she looked into his eyes. "If you have your baby here, I promise I'll protect you—if I have to sit at the foot of your bed until they release you. And you said yourself that they can't take a baby from a nursery."

She smiled as she looked at him, a momentary sparkle in her eyes and then her smile faded as they studied each other. Her lips parted while his pulse jumped. He held her chin with the tips of two of his fingers. He ached to lean the short distance between them and kiss her. He wanted her, and it shocked him each time he felt this electric tension spark between them.

It was the first time he had wanted a woman, really wanted one, since Dana. Why did it have to be this woman? *She was nine months pregnant, terrified of men and being stalked by an obsessive ex-husband!* While he stared into her wide eyes, it was difficult to remember reasons to keep his distance. His body was reacting to her, and his gaze slipped down to the baggy sweater that hid her shape completely.

He leaned back and looked at the fire. He didn't feel like talking and he knew he'd better get his thoughts off Katherine if he wanted his body to return to normal. Had she noticed the effect she had on him? He doubted it.

"Have you thought of names?" he finally asked.

"Yes. I'm trying to decide. If it's a boy, I've thought about Jacob or Cade. And if it's a girl, I like the name Emily."

"Good names."

"I'm going to court and getting my maiden name back."

"That's a good idea," he said, taking strands of her hair in his fingers and playing with them. She watched the long locks slide over his large dark-skinned hands. She suspected if she wasn't so skittish, he could touch her more. Beneath his tough exterior, he was warm and caring.

A sharp staccato rhythm ticked against the windows as sleet pelted the house. Both of them turned to look outside, and then Colin stood to go to the window.

In seconds he was back, sitting on the floor facing her again. "It's sleeting hard. The roads will be ice again."

"What will I do?"

"Let's see how it is in the morning. The weather can change here in a blink of the eye."

She stared at the window while he placed another log on the fire and watched it blaze. As they sat in easy silence, she glanced at him.

Dropping the locks of hair, he gazed into the fire, a muscle working in his jaw. Katherine felt a rush of sympathy for him. He was so strong and tough, it was amazing how vulnerable he was about losing his wife.

"You said everyone expects you to start dating. I hope you do. You're too nice to live here like a hermit."

Shifting around, Colin studied her, looking into wide, guileless green eyes, knowing if circumstances had been slightly different he would never let that statement pass. And spoken by any other woman, he would have taken it as an invitation. But as he looked at Katherine, he knew there were no hidden meanings to her words.

"Thanks. I don't think anyone ever said I was too nice to live alone. Maybe Mom, but I'm a superhero to her."

"Of course. I'd rather think of you with someone," Katherine said shyly.

And he'd rather *not* think of her with someone. And that realization startled him. It was a damn good thing the woman would be gone by this time tomorrow night.

His gaze lowered to her lips as she talked. Her mouth looked soft and inviting. Her lips were naturally rosy without lipstick, and he wanted to lean forward and brush them with his own. At the thought his body tightened, his mouth felt dry and his pulse raced. Annoyed with himself, he tore his attention from her lips to look into her eyes.

Green eyes darkened and widened, her lips parting slightly. Whatever volatile chemistry he felt around her, she had to be experiencing some kind of reaction to it, too, because there was no mistaking her response to his look. He could all but feel electricity crackle between them, yet he didn't want to do anything to break her growing trust in him. His body wanted her; his heart said to go slow and give her time. "Can I kiss you?" he whispered, unable to resist asking and wondering if he would send her flying out of the room.

"I'm not ready for that yet," she whispered in return while looking at him with an inviting gaze that made him feel as if all his nerves sizzled.

"All right. We'll work up to a kiss. Can I touch your lips with my fingers?"

She studied him solemnly and then nodded her head. "You're a very patient man."

"When it's important to be," he said softly, tracing the line of her jaw with the tips of two of his fingers. Then he ran his index finger up to the corner of her mouth. Slowly, he drew his finger over her lower lip.

His touch was as light as a feather, yet warm and tingly,

and it made her part her lips as she watched him. His gaze traveled up from her mouth.

"Okay so far?" he whispered and she nodded cautiously. She didn't feel any fear. Far from it. Her heart drummed and she tingled. She was reacting to him on a basic level, in a manner in which she hadn't reacted to a man in years. And she knew it put her on dangerous ground of another kind. This was not a man to lose her carefully guarded heart to. She needed to get to California, to get far enough away so Sloan would never follow. And she should not bring trouble to a man like Colin Whitefeather. He had already had enough trouble and heartache for a lifetime.

"Close your eyes, Katherine," Colin coaxed in a raspy voice while his dark gaze devoured her. "Let's just try a little kiss. Only for a moment."

She knew she should refuse. His dark eyes held her immobile, making her heart pound.

"Katherine," Colin whispered.

Her lashes came down, fluttered and then raised. She gave an almost imperceptible shake of her head. "I have to watch you. With my eyes shut, darkness closes in and brings old fears."

"Then you keep your eyes open," he said in a husky voice, leaning closer until he was only mere inches from her face. His dark eyes coaxed and tempted. His face was so close.

Colin's pulse raced as he leaned closer. *Be careful with her,* he reminded himself. He placed his finger beneath her chin and tilted up her face, his gaze locked with hers. His pulse drummed and he could see the blue vein throbbing in her throat and knew her pulse was racing too.

"Colin, I won't be any fun. I really—"

"Shh," he said quietly. "You're quite a woman."

As she stared into his dark eyes, her heart thudded. She

was frightened, but along with her fear was an unaccustomed warmth, a yearning that seemed to envelope her and take her breath. Strands of his black hair fell forward, framing his face while his gaze lowered to her mouth.

Her pulse sped and she felt hot, her heart fluttering. At the same time, fear taunted her, along with a need that she hadn't known she could feel. Her lips tingled. *She wanted him to kiss her.* The realization was an incredible shock. She hadn't wanted attention from any male in years. This man was tough and virtually a stranger. But she wanted him. With his gentle ways he had stirred feelings in her, yearnings that she had thought were destroyed forever.

And then Colin was so close that his face was a blur. His breath whispered against her mouth. She felt the faintest brush of his lips on hers, no more than a breeze dancing lightly over her. As her heart thudded, she closed her eyes.

His mouth brushed hers again, velvety warm, moving so slowly, heating her more than the fire. A strong arm went around her waist. She trembled, and instantly the pressure of his arm relaxed. And when he released his hold slightly, she relaxed.

His lips brushed hers a third time and heat centered in her body, longing blossoming, erasing fear. His arm made her feel safe; his lips made her feel like a desirable woman again. Her breasts tightened, her hips shifting slightly. She trembled while his arm held her firmly, and then he leaned away.

She realized his mouth was no longer on hers. She opened her eyes to find him watching her. Her pulse skittered at his heavy-lidded, smoldering gaze, which was filled with desire. Fear came racing back, but before she could do or say anything, Colin released her and turned toward the fire again.

Her momentary panic vanished as swiftly as it had come

and in its place was an intense awareness of Colin White-feather as a man. Her mouth still tingled, her body felt hot. She ached for more and she was astounded again by her reaction.

"I didn't think it was possible for me to feel what I do right now. You just gave me something back," she said, filled with wonder. She had not only wanted this man's kiss, she had relished it!

He stretched, flexing his arms and inhaling deeply, turning his head to look at her. "I didn't do anything spectacular. You were ready to be kissed."

His words, drawled in his husky voice, made her pulse race. "It was very spectacular. You're unusual, Colin Whitefeather," she said quietly.

He winked at her, something that would have annoyed her earlier, but now it seemed conspiratorial and nice. "Thanks," he said offhandedly. "I'll wonder whether you've had a boy or girl. Sometimes when I'm in town and pass that alley where you climbed into my pickup or go see my friend whose garage we hid in, I'll remember you and wonder about you. If you feel a strange tingling, maybe it'll be me thinking about you."

Colin said it lightly, yet he knew his house wasn't going to be the same for days—until memories of her faded and he settled into his solitary routine again. And that faint kiss had set him on fire. Right now he was trying to control his thoughts and his body. He wanted to haul her into his arms and kiss her until she yielded to him. Why in blazes did this woman have such an effect on him?

"I'm glad you're an ex-cop and out of the line of fire. Has anyone ever come after you out here? Have you had to shoot at anyone on your own land like you did tonight?"

"No."

Suddenly she inhaled and her eyes flew wide while she gave a little grunt.

He tilted his head to study her, wondering if she had just remembered something. "What's wrong?"

"Nothing," she said, shaking her head, but she looked preoccupied and he glanced over his shoulder almost as if he expected to see Sloan Manchester standing in the doorway with a gun on them. The room was empty except for them, and Colin turned back to look at her. She was gazing into the fire and her expression was serene again. He guessed some memory she didn't want to share had disturbed her. His curiosity satisfied, he thought about tomorrow.

"Do you have a direct flight?"

"No. It's routed through Phoenix. I should reach San Francisco about seven tomorrow night. In the morning I'll call Paula."

"Why don't you call her now?"

"I'll wait and make—" She bit off her words, suddenly squeezing her eyes closed. Her white teeth caught her lower lip. "Oh!" Her eyes flew wide open again, and he saw the same look he had seen minutes earlier.

"Katherine? What the hell?"

Six

She bit her lip and all color drained from her face as Colin realized what might be happening. "Are you having labor pains?" he asked, holding his breath as he stared at her.

Her gaze slid to the window. "I don't think so. Probably just a twinge."

"Oh, Lordy." He listened to the sleet and knew they couldn't get out if she went into labor.

"I'm all right." She bit her lip again. "Oh!"

"Katherine?"

She panted and stared at him. "That was a big twinge," she said, suddenly sounding frightened. "I have to get to California. I can't have the baby now. We can't even get to a hospital."

Katherine's hand went to her belly. She had felt her insides clench and a painful pressure contract low in her body. "Maybe it's false labor," she said, barely aware of what she was saying. The sleet drummed against the house and she knew that if the baby was coming, it would arrive here in his house because there was no way to get through the storm. They were miles from help.

"The pain is gone," she said.

He was looking at his watch. "Tell me when the next one hits," he said grimly. "I have a good doctor. He's taken care of me when I've been hurt riding and he's taken care of some of my men. He's an orthopedic and I'd trust him to recommend an obstetrician. I'll give him a call, so we'll have a name."

"Oh! There's another twinge," she said. "I want to get off the floor."

He stood and picked her up, then set her on her feet. She clutched him, her fingers biting into his arms, and Colin panicked, listening to the sleet come down. The road would be a solid sheet of ice by now and the path he had cleared today would be ice. His mind raced. "That's not even two minutes, Katherine. You're not supposed to just jump in there at less than two minutes apart. Doesn't this baby know how to come into the world?"

She opened her eyes and gasped for breath and he could tell the pain was receding. "You said you had done this before."

"Yeah, but I had paramedics show up seconds after one delivery. Shortly after the other delivery, I got the woman to the hospital. That was several years ago. And I'm no doctor," he added, feeling frightened, his mind racing on how he could get her to a hospital.

"You'll remember. Maybe I should go to the bedroom."

For a moment Katherine thought Colin was going to faint. He closed his eyes and she reached out to steady him.

Colin felt her hands hold him tightly and he jerked out of his momentary panic. She needed his help now, not his worries over being inadequate. He was no doctor, but he was going to have to deliver this baby. He thought about calling the bunkhouse, but rejected the idea. None of the men were any more experienced than he was.

"C'mon," he said tersely and was gone in an instant.

She followed him into the bedroom. He had stripped the comforter and top sheet off.

Shyness gripped her as she watched him. He was virile, sexy, attractive. And she hardly knew him, yet he was going to have to deliver her baby. Her face flushed at the thought and she looked again at the window. "We can't get through?"

"I'm calling for a med chopper and see if we can't evacuate you to Tulsa." While he grabbed the phone, she moved to the bed, standing beside it and wondering what she would have done if she had been hiding in a motel by herself or on a plane to California.

"I need a chopper. A woman is having a baby—" He paused and she turned to look at him. His expression was stormy. Then another pain racked her, her insides clenching until she forgot Colin and everything else except the pain and the wonder that her baby was finally arriving.

A spurt of warm liquid drenched her thighs and she clutched the bed, unable to do anything, burning with embarrassment. "Colin, we can't wait for a chopper. My water broke."

She heard the receiver slam down, but she didn't know what was said.

"Katherine, can you put on one of my shirts so that fuzzy sweater isn't in my way?"

She nodded and took a chambray shirt from his outstretched hands.

"As soon as you change, get into bed."

He left and she heard water running and guessed he was

washing. With shaking hands, she changed, dropping her discarded clothes in a heap. "Colin, bring a towel."

She turned to see he had already placed towels on the bed. "I'm sorry. I'll leave this all up to you."

"Forget it," he answered.

Pain came again, this time racking her body, and she clutched the bed. Colin's hands steadied her and he waited until the pain subsided, then helped her onto the bed.

"This is terrible," she said, brushing her hair away from her face. "You're not a doctor. I don't think I can get on a helicopter—"

"You won't have to until the storm stops. The chopper's being used for another emergency right now and the ice storm is presenting problems. Remember, I've done this before and they said to call if I need them and they'd tell me what to do. I'm going to get some things. You okay?"

She nodded, biting her lip, feeling the slight contractions that meant another pain was coming. It came like a wave, building until she wasn't aware of anything else. When it receded, she realized he had tossed a sheet over her.

"Can you scoot toward the foot of the bed so I can get to you easily?"

She nodded as he helped her. His hands were strong and gentle as he leaned over her and helped her move. He slipped a pillow lengthwise beneath her upper back and head.

"Colin," she whispered, clutching his hand.

He held her hand while he stared at his watch. "They're closer together. I'm calling the doc."

She didn't hear his conversation as pain enveloped her and then receded.

"I got an OB and he said as often as your contractions are, and with your water breaking, you can push when you have a contraction. This baby has definite ideas about when it's coming into the world."

The next contraction, Colin moved between her legs while he talked to someone on the telephone. As the pain mounted, she could hear him. "Push, push hard, Katherine, push!"

She panted when the pain was gone, gasping for breath, aware of the tall man between her legs, of his steady words of encouragement, dreading the next big pain, wondering if she would have a whole night of this. He talked continually on the phone, but his words didn't register with her. Finally he put aside the phone.

"Suppose there's a complication—"

She bit off her words as another contraction came and she clamped her jaw closed to muffle a cry. Her body no longer felt like her own, but was consumed by a power over which she had no control.

"Push, honey. Push hard, really hard. That's the way."

When the pain receded, she felt him bathe her forehead with a cold cloth and pat her shoulder.

"Don't worry about complications," he said. "And they said they'd call as soon as they can get a chopper through."

"Colin!"

"That's it. Grab the bed and push!"

She tried to do what he said, hanging on through a haze of pain to his strong voice, which continued to pour out encouragement.

"Okay, stop pushing. Rest now. You're doing great."

Time blurred into pain, his support, which strengthened her, and the momentary lulls when she caught her breath. She felt like screaming with the pain, but she kept her mouth clamped shut even though Colin told her to go ahead and yell if she wanted to.

After another contraction, Colin rushed around the bed to wipe her damp forehead with a cool cloth. He stroked her hair away from her face and squeezed her shoulder.

She was having this baby without anything to take the edge off the pain, without a husband or family, yet he had barely heard a whimper out of her. The contractions that tore at her made him feel faint and he wished he could do something to ease her pain. He'd rather take a beating than watch pain rack her body. He hoped his words of encouragement hid his fright.

Colin closed his eyes and said another brief prayer that this baby would be born quickly and normally. And then he saw her bite her lip and he knew another contraction was coming. He rushed back to the foot of the bed, waiting, praying complications didn't set in.

"Push! That's it, Katherine. I can see the head. Push hard. Really hard—"

His voice faded as Katherine tried to do what he said and then she felt a rush as the baby's head and shoulders were through and the powerful contraction was over.

"There you go! We've got a baby, Katherine!" he yelled exultantly. "A beautiful baby! It's a girl." In seconds he placed the baby on her belly and she gazed in amazement at the tiny infant. Not caring that the baby hadn't been cleaned yet, she stroked its face. She heard Colin talking and saw he had the phone tucked between his head and shoulder as he carefully moved the baby higher and gently kneaded her belly.

"I've cut the umbilical cord and tied it."

She realized he was getting instructions from someone. She didn't care. She had her precious baby. She looked at the tiny face and the damp red hair pressed against her head. "Emily," she whispered, joy filling her. Her gaze shifted to Colin who stood between her legs, kneading her belly and she marveled at him. He had been wonderful to her, getting her through the birth. Here she was in the most vulnerable moment of her life, and it seemed natural to have him with her and touching her.

He replaced the phone. "The chopper is on the way."

"No! I have her here now. I don't want to go—"

"You two need some official attention," he said gently, unfolding a clean sheet and draping it over her legs, placing clean towels beneath her hips and tossing the soiled bedding into a heap. He left to wash and returned, lifting her hips slightly to replace the towels on the bed with clean ones again. "Katherine, I don't have anything you need." He walked around to sit beside them. "They did tell me I can clean her up a little."

"Colin, thank you," she said, tears stinging her eyes as gratitude filled her for his gentle strength.

He smiled at her, brushing her hair back from her face as he slipped an arm beneath her shoulders and leaned down to hug her, being careful of the baby. "You were great. A very cooperative patient," he said, amazed by her strength. "You were brave, Katherine."

"I had a baby—that's natural and it doesn't have much to do with bravery."

"Oh, yes, it does," he said, straightening up and picking up the baby carefully. "I've seen men in crises or pain completely fall apart. You were brave and strong. And this is a beautiful little girl," he said. "Wait until my mother finds what I have at my house—she will pack her bags and move in here."

"I thought you said a chopper was coming."

"It is," he said without taking his eyes from the baby. "But I'll go with you. I'm getting a cop chopper from Tulsa—everyone pulled strings. They'll get you back here and then Mom will make my dad bring her here, by tractor or the horses—one way or another."

"You're a good man," Katherine said in a small voice, and Colin looked at her intently. Surprised, he saw tears brimming in her eyes.

"Hey, you don't need to cry." He bent down to kiss

her forehead. "Beautiful lady and beautiful baby," he said in a husky voice, gazing into her eyes with a warmth that made her feel cherished, even though she knew she would soon tell him goodbye and never see him again.

"Let's clean little Emily." Colin straightened and left, talking to the baby as he crossed the room.

Katherine watched him, amazed by his reaction to the baby. She would have thought a baby would have been the last thing to interest him. Instead, he was talking to her as if she understood every word he said. They disappeared into the bathroom and Katherine closed her eyes, relaxing. Her knees still shook and she was thankful she didn't have to stand up because she was certain she would fall on her face.

"Colin!" she called.

He reappeared with Emily wrapped in a large dark green towel.

"What's wrong?"

"Nothing. I just wanted to know—do you have any idea what time she was born?"

His gaze slid back to the baby. "Emily arrived in this world at exactly four minutes after midnight on February the twenty-second and I'm going to take her to the kitchen and weigh her on my fish scales."

"Fish scales?" Katherine asked, losing the thread of his conversation, staring at him as he held Emily and murmured nonsense to her. He couldn't be more taken with this baby if it had been his. He could hardly take his eyes off her.

"Scales to weigh fish I catch. It shows ounces," he explained as he was leaving the room. "And it will show you every little ounce you weigh," he said to Emily.

Katherine smiled, seeing yet another side to him, which she would never have guessed possible. She thought about earlier in the evening when he had stood in the kitchen

SARA ORWIG 93

with the rifle in his hand and looked so formidable and
tough. Now he was in the kitchen talking constantly to
Emily while he weighed her on his fish scales.

He returned, beaming, and her heart lurched. Happiness
glowed in his face and softened his rugged features. He
looked breathtakingly handsome and full of vitality. He
had caught his long hair behind his head with a strip of
leather. His blue workshirt sleeves were rolled high, revealing bulging muscles. His shirt was partially unbuttoned, giving her a glimpse of a dark-skinned muscled
chest.

He tucked the baby into Katherine's arms and sat beside
them again. "Emily weighs seven pounds and nine ounces,
a nice, respectable weight."

Katherine pushed the towel away from Emily's face.
"She hasn't cried."

"I can make her cry if you want."

"Heavens, no!"

With a flash of white teeth, he grinned. "Now I need to
get ready for a chopper."

"Colin, what will I do?"

"I'll wash your clothes, and you don't need to do anything. They'll whiz in here with a stretcher, load you and
Emily on it, whisk you out to the chopper and we'll all go
to Tulsa. Then tomorrow or whenever they release you,
I'll see to it they bring us back here."

"I don't have clothes—" she waved her hand toward
her legs.

"You're covered up and I'll put a blanket over you, but
they'll get you wrapped up. From the minute they arrive,
they'll take care of you. Stop worrying."

She tightened her arms around the infant and gazed up
at him. "Thank you, Colin."

Colin looked into her eyes and felt an intimate bond
with this woman, which he had only felt once before in

his life with Dana. He leaned down and brushed Katherine's lips lightly. "You did good, kid," he said gently, and she smiled at him.

"So did you," she answered, realizing this was one man she would never fear again.

He smiled at her as he straightened.

"Colin, I'll need my clothes at the hospital. I don't have my shoes."

"I'll take care of everything," he said, unwilling for the moment to end. He marveled at the baby, this tiny miracle who had come into the world with very little fuss and bother, all things considered. She could not help it if her mommy was running from thugs and caught in a snowstorm.

"Emily," he said softly, touching her cheek in wonder. "She's so fragile, yet I know she really isn't. She's like you—strong even though she looks so dainty and delicate."

"No one has *ever* said I look dainty or delicate. I'm five-nine, Colin," Katherine said with amusement.

"That's dainty to me," he answered.

Suddenly she caught his hand again and held it against her cheek and he saw the tears brim before she squeezed her eyes closed. "I'm so fortunate. Thank you. I thought I would go through this alone. Instead you—" She bit her lip and squeezed her eyes shut as tears brimmed over.

"Shh, Kat, don't cry. Don't cry. You have your little baby now."

She smiled, but her eyes stayed shut and tears still squeezed out beneath her long lashes. He wiped them away with his thumb.

Finally she looked up at him and wiped at her eyes. "You were wonderful to me." Her gaze shifted to Emily. "I'll name her Emily Colin."

"You'll do no such thing! Don't put a name like Colin on a beautiful little girl," he said fiercely.

Katherine looked up and smiled. "When I explain to her why she has that name, she'll be glad."

"She would never understand being named after some guy she didn't even know. Don't do that to this baby. Even my mother would agree with me on this one."

"I'll think it over."

"I better make a call," he said lightly, brushing her forehead with a kiss. Colin felt a tightening in his chest. He wanted to pull mother and baby into his arms and hold them and tell them he would protect both of them. He knew his emotions were running high because of the moment and that soon enough things would revert to normal. Giving Katherine a squeeze on the shoulder, he stood, moving around the bed to pick up the phone. As he punched the preprogrammed one-digit number, he looked at Katherine and Emily.

Katherine was propped against the pillows now, her red hair fanned out behind her head while she held Emily in the crook of her arm. For an instant he felt a pang that took his breath and almost doubled him over. They looked as if they belonged where they were and he wanted them to be there tomorrow and the day after. And then he looked at Emily and felt a rush of love that shocked him. The baby was the most beautiful child he had ever seen. He couldn't recall thinking any baby looked beautiful before Emily, but she was perfection. He wanted to take her from Katherine and hold her close.

His mother's voice broke into his thoughts.

"Mom. I have a surprise." He paused, turning to wink at Katherine. "We have a baby at my house."

"Katherine's," he answered, grinning. Katherine could hear a voice, but couldn't understand what was being said.

"I delivered her," he answered, and Katherine had to smile at the pride in his voice. "That's right."

She heard a babble of voices.

"Don't get out in the storm," Colin answered calmly. "I've called for a medical chopper—actually we're getting the police chopper and they're taking us to a Tulsa hospital. We'll probably be home tomorrow.

"Sure. As soon as we arrive. I promise I'll call you from Tulsa. Okay." He replaced the receiver and grinned at Katherine.

"Could you hear my mom? She's about to explode. She would walk over here in this storm if she thought we'd still be here." He headed toward the closet. "I better get us ready to go."

Katherine gazed at him solemnly, knowing that she should fly from Tulsa to California and never come back to his ranch. There wasn't any point in returning. A dreadful sense of loss tore at her as she watched him move around the room. He yanked his shirt out of his pants and began to unbutton it, flinging it over a chair as unselfconsciously as if they had been living together for years.

She couldn't take her gaze away. He pulled off his belt and tossed it down, moving to his dresser. Muscles rippled in his smooth back and he looked handsome and fit. He picked up a fresh pair of jeans, white briefs and went to the closet to get a shirt. "I'm going to shower. I'll be right out."

Her gaze drifted down over his sculpted chest and powerful muscles, the flat washboard stomach. He wasn't moving, she realized, and her gaze flew back up to meet his. His brows arched.

"That was a pretty thorough study for a woman who just had a baby," he drawled and winked at her and left the room.

Feeling the heat flush her face, she looked down at the

tiny baby in her arms. When she left here, she told herself again, she should go on to California from Tulsa. The planes would be flying as soon as the storm stopped and she would get her strength back quickly. She would never forget Colin Whitefeather. The thought of telling him goodbye hurt more than any beating she had taken from Sloan.

Her arms tightened around the tiny infant who dozed in her arms. Emily. Her Emily. She would think of Colin if she thought of any man in connection with this baby.

She reassured herself that she would forget the sparks Colin stirred after she was away from Oklahoma. He had been part of her life only briefly and right now she was on edge from giving birth. The world would settle and return to normal and she would forget Colin Whitefeather except as a warm memory of the man who delivered Emily.

Katherine closed her eyes, praying she did forget easily. At the moment she didn't want to leave his house or his side. She wanted his strong arms around her, his warmth and tenderness for both Emily and herself.

Yet she was vulnerable now, physically and emotionally, and Colin had momentarily stepped into a void, but he would soon vanish.

Emily Colin Manchester. That wasn't any more strange than millions of other family names, but perhaps she was overreacting. "Emily," she whispered, holding the baby tightly.

Colin reappeared from the shower and her pulse jumped. He was handsome and full of vitality. His black hair was wet, slicked back and tied with a thong of rawhide. He wore a sweatshirt and jeans that hugged his trim hips.

"I'll get things ready and call my foreman."

She closed her eyes while he talked on the phone.

"Bud, I'm leaving for the rest of the night. I should be

home tomorrow.'' He paused to listen. ''By chopper. Katherine had her baby. Yeah, I delivered her. Yeah, that's right. It's a little girl. She named her Emily.''

Katherine smiled and opened her eyes to find him watching her. He smiled again and she smiled in return. She wanted to throw her arms around his neck and she wanted him to kiss her. The notion startled her and she wondered why she would have such a reaction right after giving birth, yet she felt normal now that labor was over. And because of the delivery she felt a closeness to him she had never experienced with another person. She wanted to hold him close, just as she wanted to keep Emily in her arms.

He crossed the room to the dresser and pulled open the drawer to rummage inside. He withdrew a pistol, held it up, checking to see if it was loaded, and then tucked it into the waistband of his jeans at the small of his back. When he did, his gaze slid to her and his brows arched.

The warmth and security she had been experiencing vanished at the sight of the pistol. He gave her a level look and turned to get a knife and slip it into his boot. She felt cold, knowing she was going back into the world where danger was constant. Now she not only had to worry about herself, but she had the baby to guard.

''Stop looking so alarmed,'' he said, coming to the side of the bed. ''I told you I would protect you while you're in the hospital.''

''I shouldn't have gotten you involved in this.''

He leaned down with his hands propped on his fists on either side of her, his face close above hers. ''Don't ever worry about that again. I wouldn't have missed delivering Miss Emily for the world.''

Katherine smiled up at him and again he felt how right it seemed to have her close. He turned away abruptly. The lady had an agenda and it didn't include him. And he wasn't opening his heart to someone again.

"Colin, I should just stay in Tulsa until I can get on a plane to California and go." Katherine said it fast, as if fearful that if she didn't make her declaration quickly she wouldn't say it at all. Warmth changing to a chilly foreboding, she felt as if she was tossing away something wonderful with both hands, yet to get out of his life was the right thing to do.

He stood with his back to her, his hands in his pockets. At first she thought he hadn't heard her, but then he turned and shook his head.

"You won't be strong enough to run from those men. Not with a new baby. You come home with me until you get your strength back."

"I don't think I should."

"If I didn't want you to, I wouldn't have offered. I don't mind."

"It isn't just the danger," she said hesitantly. Her green eyes were wide and guileless. Pink suffused her face. "I feel something when I'm around you."

"Are you afraid of falling in love again?" he asked bluntly. As he waited for her answer, he held his breath.

"No! I'm going to California to start over."

"There you have it," he said, breathing again, trying to ignore a nagging sense of disappointment. Telling himself to be glad about her answer—he knew he had no place in his life for her. Not on a permanent basis.

"You're not ready for love in your life," he continued. "I'm sure as hell not," he added gruffly. "I won't ever open my heart to that kind of hurt again. Not ever," he said, his dark eyes boring into her.

As Katherine watched him, she felt he was trying to tell her not to expect anything from him.

He moved to the window and stared outside. "So there's

no reason for you to avoid coming back here for a time. You won't inconvenience me too much, and I can protect you. And then you can go.''

She looked at his broad shoulders and felt a longing for something she felt she had missed. She had been infatuated with Sloan and she had rushed headlong into marriage too young. From the start it had not been good. He had been unfaithful and had lied to her. She'd hoped to salvage their marriage until she realized there wasn't anything to salvage. There had never been any real love or companionship between them. Never once during those years had there been the warmth and intimacy she had felt tonight with Colin Whitefeather. He was a unique man, and she hoped someday he would fall in love again.

And when that finally happened, Katherine knew, the woman would be very, very lucky. "Colin, how old are you?''

"Thirty-one.'' He tilted his head to one side and looked out the window. "I hear the chopper.''

She didn't hear anything, but Colin left the room and in minutes she heard a clacking noise, which grew louder and louder outside. Soon there were voices in the next room, doors banging, and then cops and an off-duty paramedic swarmed the bedroom.

Colin followed them inside while they worked to get Katherine on a stretcher. Colin pulled on his shearling coat and placed his hat on the back of his head. He was rummaging in his drawer for gloves when he heard Katherine's voice.

"No! She's stays with me.''

He turned around, because he had never heard her use that tone of voice with him.

"Yes ma'am.'' The paramedic who was over six feet tall straightened and took a step back from the bed as he looked down at Katherine, holding Emily in her arms.

Colin looked at Katherine's green eyes and knew why the man had backed off. Amused, he realized his assessment of her last night had missed the mark. He had thought she was fragile. All the time since he met her, he had felt protective of her. She had seemed frightened, uncertain and frail. One look at the fire in her green eyes and he realized beneath all her obvious needs, this was one tough lady. He had seen men look less fierce when they were going for their guns. It was little Emily who brought out the tough streak in her mommy.

Katherine's gaze shifted to him. He winked and gave her a thumbs-up before he turned away.

In a short time they were off in the helicopter, swooping over his land and rising in the night sky.

Colin glanced down at the snowy landscape, dotted with dark cedars. He hoped the men who were after her were close and saw the chopper leave. They might think she was out of the place for good.

He turned back to look at the tiny baby. He felt possessive toward her and he told himself that was absurd. He was no part of her and had no claim on her. In spite of his logical arguments, he wanted to hold her. Annoyed with himself, he shifted his gaze, meeting Katherine's steady stare. She looked away and he remembered the moment he had so lightly kissed her, kisses that he should have forgotten. They were so faint they shouldn't have been so sexy or memorable, but they were both.

Running his hand over his head, he wondered how Katherine had gotten past so many barricades to his heart. He could just put her on the plane in Tulsa and never take them back home with him. She wouldn't object. It was the intelligent thing to do, if he didn't want to run risks of getting hurt again.

Katherine watched him, wondering what he was thinking, feeling as if she had just flown away from the only true home she had known since childhood. She tightened her arm around her sleeping baby and then reached out her other hand to Colin, who closed his big fingers around hers immediately.

When they reached the Tulsa hospital she and Emily were whisked away while he took care of the admitting formalities.

When he finished, he settled in an empty waiting room. He paced the floor and then sat down, poking through magazines, picking up an old issue and thumbing through it. A picture caught his attention and he turned back. Names in the news and pictures of various politicians were spread over two pages. He looked again at the name that had caught his attention and then at the picture above it.

He had seen Sloan Manchester on television and had a vague memory of what the man looked like. Now Colin took a good look. Sloan was smiling into the camera and waving at an audience. Anger knotted in Colin as he gazed at the picture. The man was probably what women would consider a gorgeous hunk of man. Sloan was taller than the men around him, had a thick mop of golden hair and even white teeth with a dimple in his cheek. He had rugged good looks, a deceptively wholesome appearance.

Colin realized he was crushing the magazine in his fists and he relaxed his hold as he continued to stare at the picture. Someone should stop Manchester from running for governor. Someone should blow the whistle on the bastard.

Disgusted, Colin tossed the magazine back onto the table and stood up to pace again.

Finally a nurse called to him. "Mr. Whitefeather. Katherine is settled in her room, if you'd like to see her."

He rode in the elevator, the thought nagging him that he should put her on the plane. She was strong and could make it to California, and then she would be safe. And out of his life. He wouldn't risk getting shot at when he went home. He wouldn't have to constantly be on watch and worry about his men getting hurt. Or his parents. And he wouldn't have to battle his conscience over Katherine. If she came home with him and stayed any time at all, sooner or later, he knew he would make a pass at her. She was a beautiful, appealing woman.

She was also an adult who could make her own decisions, he reminded himself.

Send her on her way and stay out of trouble. She'll be happy as soon as she reaches California. He knew he would be glad to settle back into his routine. Although, every time he thought about getting his life back to normal, it was unsettling. He was going to miss Katherine. Without any fanfare or fuss, she had become part of his life.

The elevator door opened and two men stepped on. They were riding to the next floor and Colin spread his feet, studying them obliquely and swiftly, deciding he could relax. He had been ready to go for his pistol if it had been necessary, but on the next floor they got off.

Let her go. If he just put her on the plane to California, he could forget about Katherine and Emily and men who might shoot at him.

Colin pushed open the door, closing it quietly behind him. Katherine was asleep, with Emily in a small bassinet nearby. Colin tiptoed to look at Emily, marveling again at the tiny baby he had helped bring into the world. Her fingers were doubled into small fists, her arms thrown up over her head while she slept propped on her side with a pillow rolled behind her. He touched her soft cheek, wondering about her, imagining a little girl with long red hair and big green eyes, a tiny version of Katherine. He felt a tightening in his chest and he wanted to pick her up and hold her close, and he understood Katherine's fierce protectiveness.

He leaned down to brush a kiss on the top of her head

and caught the smell of lotion and soap. "Sweet Emily," he whispered.

He turned and looked at the still form on the bed. He moved close to stand with his knee touching the bed. Katherine was on her back, one arm flung out, her red hair spilling over her shoulders. His gaze traveled down over the hospital gown, the sheet that was across her hips and legs. He drew a deep breath. All his tender feelings stirred by the sight of the baby, transformed to desire for the sleeping woman.

He wanted to lean down and pull her into his arms. While fantasies danced in his mind, he went to the window. He opened the blinds a fraction to look at the cars covered in snow in the brightly lit parking lot. Had the men followed them to Tulsa? They wouldn't have been able to keep up with the chopper, but it wouldn't be difficult to guess what had happened. There weren't any chopper taxi services in this part of the country. Chances were, the men had assumed she had had her baby and was in a Tulsa hospital, since the chopper had left in that direction. Were they watching the airport?

He moved to a chair, placing it closer to the bassinet, not trusting himself to sit too close to Katherine. He propped his booted feet on a table, settled back and closed his eyes, falling asleep instantly.

A whisper of sound brought Colin awake. He stood and spun around, his hand going to his back for his pistol.

Seven

"Sorry!" Colin swore silently as he threw up his hands. He faced a frowning nurse who held a paper cup in her hand. "I was asleep and you startled me." She continued to stare at him. "I'll get out of the way," he said swiftly, rushing past her and into the hall.

Colin left, going to get breakfast, making a phone call to the ranch and to the station to talk to Simms. Next he rented a Jeep to run errands. It was over an hour later when he returned to the hospital with his arms laden with packages.

The room was quiet again and he placed sacks and boxes carefully on a chair. He poked through them and finally found what he wanted, pulling a fluffy pink bunny from a sack and placing it at the foot of the bassinet. After spending several minutes looking at Emily, Colin settled in a chair.

As he sat down, Katherine stirred. She stretched languidly, a fluid motion of her body and long legs beneath the sheet while she flung out her arms. Her eyes opened slowly and focused on him and a smile curved her full lips.

Watching her, Colin felt on fire. Her slight movements had been seductive, her smile was fiery temptation. Her arm was outflung, the back of her hand against the bed. She curled her fingers, motioning to him to come close.

He could not have resisted if his life had depended on it. He felt as if he were burning in the heat of green fires in her steady gaze. He stood and moved to the side of the bed. She caught his hand in hers and rubbed it against her cheek. "Thank you again for last night," she said softly.

His thoughts were far from the previous night. He struggled with himself. His body was reacting to her and he wanted to slide into bed with her and pull her into his arms, to fit her against him and feel her long legs wrap around him.

Unable to speak, knowing he had to move away before she saw how he was responding, he kissed her cheek lightly and turned to walk to the bassinet to look at Emily.

"Isn't she pretty?" Katherine said brightly behind him, and he heard the rustle of the covers. He didn't trust himself to turn around yet and he couldn't answer. He suspected if he tried to talk, his voice would be a hoarse croak. He leaned down to look closer at the sleeping baby and finally he turned.

"She's the prettiest baby I've ever seen."

"Liar!" Katherine laughed. She had raised the head of the bed and sat up, smiling at him. "Colin, what's that in the bassinet?"

"It's Emily's first toy," he said proudly, holding up the fuzzy rabbit while Katherine's smile widened.

"That's nice of you. Dr. Southridge said she's perfect. Well, he actually said she's in fine shape and very healthy and your scales must have been right because he gave me the same weight you did."

"And how about Emily's mama? I wanted to talk to the doc."

"You'll get your chance. Dr. Southridge is a pediatrician. Colin, my purse is in the closet. Can you please hand it to me?"

He found the purse and brought it back to the bed. "I don't think the hospital administration would be thrilled to know you're packing a pistol."

"They'll never know." She looked in the purse. "I don't want to have any fuss from you. I want to pay for what I can." She pulled out a wad of bills that made him draw a deep breath. His hand closed over hers tightly.

"Damnation. It's a wonder someone hasn't mugged you. You shouldn't carry money like that around! It shouldn't be lying around here—too many people come and go in this room."

"I have to carry cash. I can't draw any money from a bank. Sloan will have seen to that. Besides, cash doesn't leave a paper trail. Now—" She looked up at him because he still had his hand tightly over hers.

He leaned down to look her in the eye. "You're not paying a cent. Put this money away."

They stared at each other in a silent contest of wills.

"Katherine, I'm going to get my way here."

She clamped her lips together and stuffed the money back into her purse. She sighed. "Thank you."

"One more thing. I thought you might want some clothes. I don't know whether I have the right sizes. I took your old clothes and had a clerk pick these things out." He placed boxes and sacks on the bed.

"Now you have to let me pay you."

"No, I don't have to."

"Are we going to ruin our friendship with a fight?"

"No, we're not. I'm doing what I wanted to do. Consider it all a gift for Emily."

"You have a stubborn streak, Colin."

"Could be."

She glared at him a moment and then opened a sack and pulled out a red sweater. She smiled at him. "How'd you guess I love red?"

"Intuition," he lied, wondering if she would like it or want something else because of her red hair.

She opened another box and pulled out a pair of jeans. She looked at the waist and sighed. "I may not be able to fasten these."

"I'm guessing you can."

She picked up a fancy white sack and turned it in her hands. "This looks interesting."

"I told you. A nice lady clerk picked things out for me. I didn't select anything except the red sweater."

Katherine opened the sack and looked at a bit of purple lace. She glanced at him. "You don't know what's in this sack?"

His dark eyes gave her an answer before he spoke. "I know what's in there. I bought it. She helped with my selection."

Katherine thought about the plain cotton bras she had worn for a long time because she had not wanted to look appealing to Sloan. The purple lace was sensuous and the thought of Colin deciding to buy it for her made her blush. With care she moved it and beneath it found more substantial bras. Without taking them from the sack, she turned them, realizing he had brought her some nursing bras.

"Exactly what I needed," she exclaimed, glancing at him. Beneath them was more lace and she moved the bras aside to see a pair of lacy purple panties and a lacy red pair.

"I suppose it's needless to say you shouldn't have."

"Absolutely. I keep telling you, I did what I wanted."

Two more boxes were on the bed. She picked up the smaller one and opened it to find a tiny dress with embroidery and pink ruffles. A pair of pink booties were with it and a small pink cap.

"Colin, this is like Christmas!" she said, holding up the dress. "It's beautiful and Emily will look like a doll in it. Thank you!"

"You're welcome."

She put the dress away carefully and pulled the last box onto her lap. It was a large white box that was from the same store as the sack with the lingerie, and she wondered what else he had bought. She raised the lid and drew a deep breath as she looked at a silky red nightgown and peignoir.

"Thank you!"

"You're welcome. If the jeans don't fit, I can exchange them. Also, I got little Emily a few things she'll need."

He produced an infant carrier that was filled with diapers and gowns and bottles.

"Colin, you shouldn't do all this."

He set the carrier aside. "I'm enjoying myself. If—" He paused at a knock on the door and stood as a white-coated physician entered the room.

"I'm Dr. Deke Lowery," the dark-haired man said, extending his hand.

"I'm Colin Whitefeather."

"You did the delivery. Very good. Mother and baby are fine."

"I hope I don't have to do that again. I'll wait outside while you check them." Colin stepped outside and waited. When the physician emerged from the room, Colin reached out to close the door behind him.

"I have some questions. Can she take the baby and travel on a plane this week to California?"

Deke Lowery studied Colin and shook his head. "I wouldn't recommend it. The lady's lost blood and she's weak. But if it's absolutely necessary that she travel, she'll survive. She's healthy and strong and so is the baby."

"So she can fly to California?"

"Yes, she can. But I don't think she should."

Colin nodded his head. "If I take her home with me, how soon can we leave here?"

"You'll be home to help her?"

"If I'm not, my mother will."

"I can sign a release now."

"Let's do that."

Colin knew he could never put them on a plane. If the men were watching the airports, she wouldn't stand a chance of getting away from them once she left his side. Not in the condition she was in now and carrying Emily. He would take her home with him. He watched a nurse go into her room and he stepped across the hall to a phone. He stood where he could watch Katherine's door while he called his mother to tell her they were coming home.

The next week Colin's life was turned upside down. His mother moved in and his father came by every day. Katherine seemed to blossom, appearing at breakfast in one of his mother's cotton robes, during the day wearing a sweater of his mother's and a pair of his mother's slacks. His father arrived each day with bundles in his arms. Now Colin's old cradle was in the bedroom and his old high chair was in the kitchen, something Emily could not possibly use for another six months. His mother slept in his bedroom on a cot, while Katherine had his bed and he slept on the sofa.

The first day he cautioned his mother about answering

the phone. That night after she had gone to bed, Katherine sat quietly rocking a sleeping Emily.

"The phone rang today."

"Anyone answer?"

"No. There wasn't any message. Just a long silence. That happened several times."

"They're checking, trying to learn whether or not you're still here. As long as you and Mom don't answer, there's no way for anyone to know. If they're watching with binoculars, they can't see anything."

"Not until I leave."

"They may give up after a time and try to pick up the trail elsewhere."

"Don't you think they can find out about us being at the hospital?"

"If they're good, yes."

"And then they'll learn that I came back here with you."

"So you wait and be careful and when the time comes, I'll help get you out of here. We'll get plane tickets to several cities at the same time. Send them off on wild chases."

She nodded and stood. "I'll put Emily to bed. Colin, your mother asked me to write to her and send her pictures of Emily."

He felt another twist of hurt. "She wants a grandchild. I think she realizes this is as close as she'll ever get to having one. I won't marry again."

"You don't know that!" Katherine snapped. "You might change your mind, Colin. You're too warm and loving—"

"I don't *want* to marry," he said harshly. "It's like hocking your heart." Restless, he moved to the hearth to place another log on the fire. "I won't put myself through that pain again."

Katherine knew he hurt and it pained her. He seemed strong and invincible, yet in his heart he was vulnerable. And Nadine Whitefeather already adored Emily. She was meant to have grandchildren and Colin was wonderful with Emily. "I'm sorry about your loss."

"Yeah," he said, running his hand over his hair. "I guess we're all babes in arms in one way or another—me, you, little Emily. Even my mother. We're vulnerable to hurt."

"You won't always be, Colin. You'll heal."

He shot her a stormy look and stood abruptly. "I'm going out to see about the dogs."

Katherine watched him stride across the room. In the kitchen he yanked on his coat and hat and she suspected he would be outside a long time. She hugged Emily, placing her cheek against the warm baby, aching for Colin and wishing she could put her arms around him.

The days became weeks, and they settled into a routine. The chilly winter transformed into a blustery March with winds sweeping across the land and buffeting the house.

Colin realized on the surface everything seemed rosy, yet he knew phone calls were coming in daily and no one would speak on the other end of the line. He was aware that Katherine was growing more tense as she regained her strength. And he was edgier because he was thrown with her constantly in intimate situations. The house was too small to avoid brushing against each other, to avoid seeing her come out of the bathroom wrapped in a towel, to catch her nursing Emily, modestly covered, yet on occasion he had caught a tantalizing glimpse of the curve of her breast. And he knew beneath her happiness, his mother feared the moment Katherine and Emily would go.

During the sixth week at a 2:00 a.m. feeding, Emily was fussy. Katherine stepped into the living room. Colin sat up, shaking his hair back from his face, staring through the darkness at her. "Trouble?"

"I don't know whether she's colicky or what. I didn't want her to wake your mother."

He gave a grunt as he reached for his jeans and yanked them on. "Mom would probably rather you'd wake her. And she might know what's wrong."

"I'll try walking Emily for a while."

"I'll walk her," he said, crossing the room to take Emily from her.

He had been busy buttoning his jeans and he looked up to find Katherine staring at him. His chest was bare, the top button still unfastened to his jeans. Her gaze wandered over him, and his pulse jumped and his heart pounded as he looked at her with the same blatant curiosity.

Her hair fell over her shoulders. The cotton robe was open and he saw she was wearing a cotton gown his mother must have brought over.

"Where's the red nightgown I bought?"

She tugged at her collar. "It's so fancy and your mother brought some gowns that seem practical when Emily might spit up on me. And these are less revealing. I love your gift, Colin."

Barely aware of her answer, he moved closer to take the baby, yet he couldn't take his eyes off Katherine, looking down at her intently. He wanted her, and he wondered if his hormones had gone into overdrive after being so long dormant.

Katherine handed Emily to him and he placed her against his shoulder while Katherine moved to a chair.

"Go on back to bed," he said, his voice hoarse. "I'll take care of her." He began to walk and pat Emily on the back while she cried. In seconds, her crying subsided and then she snuggled against him. He held her close while he walked back and forth and talked softly to her. He saw the bedroom door close and knew Katherine had gone to bed.

Emily was quiet and he shifted her into his arms, looking down at her. She stirred and whimpered and he placed her on his shoulder again. He sat in the rocker and slowly rocked, finally propping his feet up and putting his head back to doze.

He woke when the first faint rays of sun shone in the room. Emily was sleeping quietly and he stood, carrying her carefully to her bed.

His mother was under a mound of covers on the cot. Katherine sat up in bed and he straightened, pointing at Emily. Once again he was immobilized momentarily by the sight of Katherine who looked disheveled and tempting, the worn cotton gown clinging to her figure, revealing her full breasts.

He turned abruptly and left the room.

The next night after supper they all sat around the fire. It was April now, and hints of spring were in the air, yet the nights often remained chilly. His father had joined them to eat and he played with Emily who stared at him while she waved her fists in the air. When she whimpered, he stood to place her in Nadine's lap.

"She's all yours, Mother."

"I wish she were," she said, smoothing Emily's hair. "I think it's time I go back home with you tonight, Will."

"It is about time I got a little attention," Will said good-naturedly as she stood to hand Emily to Colin.

"I'm so proud of you, Colin. To think you delivered her—that's wonderful."

"I think so, too," Katherine said, smiling at him.

Colin jiggled and patted Emily while Nadine carried dishes to the sink.

"I'll come back tomorrow, so I'll leave some of my things."

Later, after cleaning the kitchen and talking a while, they walked to the door. Colin's folks pulled on coats and gloves. Finally Nadine turned to take Emily again to hug her. "This is the most beautiful baby I've ever seen!"

"I think so, too," Katherine said.

"What about Colin?" Will asked, grinning.

"Colin was a handsome little boy, but he wasn't beautiful. Emily is beautiful." She kissed Emily's cheek and handed her back to Colin.

Suddenly Katherine stepped forward to hug Nadine. "Thank you for coming over and helping. You've been wonderful to us."

They hugged each other, and Colin saw tears in his mother's eyes.

"Mom, you'll be back tomorrow."

"I know."

Knowing it wasn't tomorrow that worried her, Colin followed them outside, a brisk breeze nipping at him as he scanned the horizon, looking at the lit grounds around the barn and bunkhouse.

As soon as his folks had driven away, he stepped inside and locked the door. "After they're gone, I'll reset the alarm."

Katherine was aware of the intimacy of being alone with Colin. "I put Emily in her bed. Your mother has been great."

It seemed natural for Colin to drape his arm across Katherine's shoulders as they walked back into the living room. He realized she had lost her fear of him. Suddenly he became intensely aware of her hip brushing his, the scent of roses about her, the way she fit under his arm. He wanted her with an intensity that rippled through him and made his body tighten. He dropped his arm and moved away abruptly.

He built a fire, made hot chocolate and sat and talked with Katherine until they heard Emily's cries.

"Feeding time," Katherine said.

"Bring her in here. You can have the rocker." He sat on the floor with his arms around his knees, his legs drawn up. The rocker was behind him and in dark shadows. He had long ago turned off the lights and the only light in the room was from the fire. Katherine would be in shadow, behind him, and she would have her privacy, but he didn't know whether she would return or not. In minutes he heard a rustle behind him and knew she was back.

"Think your mother will be here early tomorrow?"

"Probably. There's still enough ice and snow that Dad will bring her before he's off to do his chores. I think she wants every second she can get with Emily. I know Dad's glad to have her home. He doesn't like being without her."

"Then they have a good marriage."

"Yes, they do." Colin rested back on his elbows, stretching out his legs, his mind half on their conversation while he thought about Katherine. He could hear her steadily rocking, and after a while he knew Emily had to be sleeping.

He glanced over his shoulder. "She asleep?"

"Yes."

He stood and went to take the sleeping baby from her, carrying her to the tiny cradle and settling her on her side. He returned to find Katherine still rocking, gazing into the fire. He crossed the room to her and took her hand, pulling her to her feet. Her brows arched in question as she looked up at him.

"It's good to have you here," he said in a husky voice.

Katherine's heart jumped as she watched him solemnly. The room was in shadow and she couldn't see the expression on his face. Her pulse drummed while he held her hand lightly.

"You're not afraid any longer, are you?"

She shook her head. "No. But I can't tell you at what point my fears will return. Even if they are irrational."

"Let's see how we're doing," he said softly, sliding his arm around her waist and drawing her closer with deliberation. Her heart thudded and her lips tingled. Anticipation rocked her as she closed her eyes and tilted her head up.

Colin's mouth covered hers, his tongue thrusting into her mouth. Desire heated her as she moaned softly and swayed toward him. His arm tightened around her, fitting her to his length while he wound his other hand in her hair.

His kiss deepened, became more demanding. To her amazement, she wanted him, wanted his kisses. Fear was gone, memories vanished. This powerful man had brought about more than one miracle in her life and she marveled at it on one level, while on another physical level she responded fully for the first time in years.

Colin leaned over her as he felt her response. His heart hammered violently and he wanted Katherine with a need that made him shake. And he knew it was impossible. She had to go on her way soon. She would walk out of his life forever and that was the way they both wanted it, but right now he wanted to hold and touch and kiss her so badly, he was willing to run some risks of being hurt.

And he knew it was going to hurt badly when he put Katherine and Emily on a plane. He closed his thoughts to their parting, holding her close, reassuring himself that she was in his arms and returning his kisses now. He slid his hand across her back, knowing her so intimately in some ways, barely knowing her at all in others.

His hand slipped around her waist, which had already changed drastically. His fingers pushed beneath her sweater and moved upward. He cupped her breast, feeling the practical cotton bra. Impatiently, he shifted, moving to free the clasp.

Katherine wound her arms around his neck while she returned his kisses. It was obvious he wanted her and in a few minutes she would have to stop him, but for now, she wanted to be held and kissed, to feel like a complete, desirable woman.

He pushed away her bra and then his hand cupped her breast once more, his thumb caressing her tender nipple. She gasped with pleasure as desire burned like fire in her body.

She melted against him, fitting her body to his hard length, feeling his manhood press against her belly. She had never expected to feel desire again, to ache and want a man to caress and kiss her, and amazement mingled with longing.

Colin caught the hem of her sweater and pulled it over her head, tossing it down.

"Colin," she finally protested, feeling torn between wanting what she might never have a chance for again and knowing they should stop before they brought more pain to themselves.

"Just a few kisses," he whispered. "I know you're going. Just a little loving, Katherine. So little," he coaxed, his hands moving over her soft skin, cupping her breasts. She closed her eyes and moaned, her hands sliding down to his strong arms as he pushed her away slightly. His dark gaze studied her and she trembled from the hunger that burned in his expression. His gaze traveled over her slowly, lowering to her breasts and then he leaned down to take her nipple in his mouth.

"Lord, you're beautiful!" he whispered, one hand stroking her back while his other hand held her waist.

She clung to him, her eyes squeezed shut as she ran her fingers through his thick hair. His words danced in her heart, a song that she would treasure always. She had never felt delicate and beautiful, not like Colin made her feel, and she wanted to touch and kiss him in return. She wanted to toss all caution and wisdom aside and take what the moment offered, storing up a memory to hold through the long, lonely years ahead.

She wound her fingers in his hair. "Colin," she whispered, wanting to tell him he was special, yet unable to speak. His tongue flicked over her nipple, his teeth closing gently while fire streaked in her.

She wanted to sink to the floor, spread her legs and pull him to her, but it was too soon for her body, far too soon for her heart. "Colin, I have to stop—"

Instantly he straightened up, pausing. Then he pulled her close to bend down and kiss her as if it were the last kiss he would ever have. His demanding mouth took her breath, making her heart pound while her hips moved against him as if she couldn't control her body.

He stopped abruptly, releasing her. "I'm going out, Katherine," he said, leaving the room.

Startled by his abrupt departure, she wondered if she had hurt or angered him. "Colin—"

He turned at the door. Firelight flickered over him and she saw the bulge in his jeans that told her whatever caused him to go so abruptly, he wanted her.

"I didn't mean to—" She stopped, not knowing what to say. "I just thought we should stop before things got out of hand."

"Yeah," he said gruffly, and she saw the warm, tenderhearted man hidden once again behind the tough-cop exterior. He left, and the back door slammed behind him.

She pulled her bra back on and picked up her sweater, going to the bedroom. She changed into a nightgown and climbed into bed. She wondered about Colin. Was he still outside? Had he been angry with her or merely trying to exercise control? She shivered, hoping he wasn't angry.

The first week they were back from the hospital he had wrung a promise from her to stay until he could take her back to see the doctor at the end of six weeks. Both Emily and she could have a checkup and then, Colin said, he would put them on the plane. Her appointment was in three days. It hurt to think of going and she closed her eyes, remembering his arms around her and his kisses that made her ache to be with him. Three days and she would have to tell him goodbye.

She couldn't sleep, and after half an hour of tossing and turning she got out of bed. She looked at Emily who was peacefully sleeping and then went to the window, her gaze scanning the landscape. The April night was dark, with only a sliver of moon in the sky. A shadow moved and her heart lurched and then calmed as she recognized the silhouette of Colin's broad shoulders and his wide-brimmed hat. The dogs were at his heels and he stood on the road, staring into the night. He was a solitary figure and she thought about him staying in this house by himself.

Longing tore at her, making her want to grab a coat and shoes and go out and get him and bring him back into the warmth of the house. Into the rapture of each other's arms. She liked Colin's kisses. She liked having him hold and caress her—something she would not have thought possible only a short time ago.

"Colin, come inside," she whispered, her breath frosting the glass so she could no longer see him. She moved over, to look out the next window. He stood with his hands on his hips as if confronting something, looking down the road. Was he trying to see someone? Or was he lost in his thoughts. Or was he fighting demons of his own?

She stood for another half hour, watching him, waiting,

until he finally turned and walked to the barn and disappeared inside. Was he going to sleep in the barn? Had she disturbed his life that much?

She moved back to bed, stretching out, knowing she should sleep while Emily slept. Katherine closed her eyes and gave herself over to tormenting memories of Colin's kisses.

The next morning as Katherine entered the kitchen, Colin stepped in the back door. He had a smudge of dirt on his cheek, but he looked fresh and alert and incredibly handsome. She wanted to run throw herself into his arms, but she knew she couldn't.

"Good morning. Where's our little girl?"

Katherine's heart jumped and she stared at him, momentarily taken aback by his question, then realizing he had spoken casually and meant nothing personal. "She just went back to sleep."

"Shucks. I wanted to see her." He hung his hat and coat on a peg and turned to cross the room. "Almost as much as I wanted to see her mommy," he said, placing his hands lightly on Katherine's shoulders.

Her pulse jumped wildly and she gazed up at him. "I thought you'd be hard at work."

He leaned down to kiss her neck. "I'm hard in the kitchen, and it's because of a beautiful redhead."

"You know what I meant!" she said, twisting away from him, knowing if she didn't she might turn and give herself to him completely. She moved to the refrigerator to get out orange juice and pour herself a glass. "Want some?" She glanced over her shoulder at him and her pulse did another erratic skitter as Colin's gaze ran languidly over her in a basic male assessment.

"I definitely want some," he drawled, and she forgot the orange juice.

"Colin—"

He crossed the kitchen, his gaze locked on hers, his purpose as clear in his hot expression as if he had stated it.

Her heart pounded and she set down the pitcher. Her mouth went dry and she couldn't protest or say anything. She stood watching him as he walked up and wrapped his arms around her.

"I don't ever want to frighten you," he said in a husky, solemn voice.

"You won't. You've worked a miracle, Colin. I didn't think I would ever be normal again or have normal reactions. I trust you completely," she said and something flickered in the depths of his eyes, as if she had hurt him.

His hand wound in her hair and he pulled her close, resting his chin on the top of her head. "You trust me completely," he repeated, and she wondered if she had placed an impossible barrier between them.

She shifted slightly and studied him, looking into his dark eyes, which held no promises but were filled with desire. She placed her hands on his jaw and drew his head down. Standing on tiptoe, she kissed him, her tongue entering his mouth, touching his tongue.

His arms tightened around her into bands that made her feel desired. He kissed her hard, bending over her and pressing his hand against the small of her back to hold her close against him.

She slipped her arms around his neck and held him tightly, clinging to him. She kissed him and was kissed in return, wanting him badly, knowing now he was worrying about hurting her emotionally. And probably trying to keep barriers up around his own emotions.

She wanted to cry out to him to let go his hurt, to open his heart and love again, but she knew she had no right to say those things to him when she was walking out of his life. And there wasn't a choice, even if he wanted her to stay. She would bring trouble and Sloan's wrath on any man she was involved with at this point in her life. And she was still far too close to Sloan.

Something hurt deep inside, a different kind of hurt that she had not known before. It was an ache for Colin, for what might have been and could not be between them. Yet what were a few harmless kisses? She held him close, feeling his heart race as much as hers was racing while she kissed him hungrily.

Colin's hands slipped over her, sliding down to cup her round bottom and pull her up against him, his hard shaft pressing between them. She was fire in his blood, awakening needs. *"I trust you completely."* The words played in his mind, tormenting him while he kissed her and ached to carry her to bed now. *I trust you....*

He couldn't break that trust. He could offer her no promises, no future. He couldn't give her love. And the knowledge that someday she would find love made his arms tighten around her as if he could hold her and keep her for himself without any promises.

His hand slipped beneath her sweater, unfastening her bra swiftly, cupping her buttery softness, which made him tremble for control. He shoved aside the sweater, taking her full, milky breast in his mouth, flicking his tongue over her taut nipple while her hips thrust against him.

He kissed her hungrily, stroking her back, feeling the curve at her waist. His hands went to the buttons on her jeans. She caught his wrist.

"Colin—"

The word was a warning and he knew with this woman he must stop the moment she wanted him to stop. He straightened up to gaze down at her, wanting her, aware how impossible a relationship between them was. Fires danced in her green eyes and their flames burned his heart.

He inhaled deeply and turned to walk away from her. He couldn't trust himself to speak, moving across the kitchen to the pegs that held his hat and coat. Without looking at her, he struggled for control. "I thought I'd come back and have breakfast with you. Maybe it wasn't such a good idea."

"Sit down. You have to eat to work."

He yanked down his coat and hat, pulling on the heavy coat. He turned around. "I know what I want. I'll eat later, when I can keep my hands to myself." He left, striding across the yard.

Startled, Katherine went to the back door to watch him. Aching, she wanted to love and hold him. She wanted his fierce loving, which would all but consume her, yet would make her feel desirable. His long-legged stride ate up the ground. His black hair was loose over his shoulders, giving him a rugged, wild appearance and she could imagine his Comanche ancestors and wondered if any of them were as gentle at heart as Colin.

She turned inside, going to the counter to pour a steaming cup of black coffee. Two more days and she and Emily would have to get out of his life forever.

Midmorning her plans changed. The phone rang and she waited, pausing by the answering machine while she folded Emily's clothes, which she had just taken out of the dryer. The voice that came over the machine startled her. She jumped and dropped the gown in her hands.

"Katherine." Sloan's voice was deep and clear and unmistakable.

"I know you're there. Pick up the phone."

Eight

There was a moment of silence while she looked at the phone. She felt as if an icy wind had taken all the warmth from the room.

"All right," he continued. "You won't pick up the phone, but you're standing there listening to me."

She jumped again and looked over her shoulder at the windows, as if she might see him in the yard or standing at a window, looking inside at her. Hairs on the nape of her neck rose and her skin prickled. Frightened, she felt as if he could see her, and she moved along the counter away from the phone.

"I'm bringing you home. Don't fight me when I come for you. Don't bring trouble down on someone who is no part of our lives. You're going to cause innocent people to get hurt if you keep hiding behind them. We can work out our differences."

Another pause of silence came. "We'll take the baby

home. Dad and I hoped you would have a boy to carry on
our name, but once again you disappointed me. I'll see
you soon. Don't let others get hurt because of your foolishness.''

The phone clicked and the room was silent.

How far away was Sloan? Did he really know she was
standing close, listening to his message? He knew about
Emily's birth. Katherine shivered. And he was warning her
he would hurt Colin if Colin got in the way.

And she knew Colin would get very much in the way.
She had to go now before Colin got back. She had to take
Emily and get out of Colin's life so he didn't get hurt. He
was innocent in this battle she had with Sloan and he
shouldn't be hurt by it. And if he were hurt, Nadine and
Will Whitefeather could be hurt, too.

Katherine rushed to the bedroom and yanked out her
leather handbag. Looking around the room, she felt dis-
may. How would she cram Emily's things into the bag?
Her diapers alone could fill more than the bag.

She ran out to the garage and climbed to the attic. The
moment she stepped into the attic, she found what she
hoped would be there—suitcases. She took one and went
downstairs to load it and the bag. It would be conspicuous,
but if she moved quickly now maybe she could get a head
start on Sloan.

Emily was asleep, her hands doubled into fists, and
Katherine did not want to wake her until the last possible
moment. She gathered her things, packing swiftly, finally
going to the kitchen to sit down and write a note to Colin.

Dear Colin:
Thank you for everything. I will never forget you.
Thank your mom and dad for being so wonderful. I
wish Emily could know all of you as she grows up.
I am taking your Jeep to the airport and will

leave it in the airport parking lot. I will send your suitcase, coat and hat back to you and the baby clothes that were once yours, which your mother brought over.

Katherine reread the note. She hurt so badly, aching, looking at the place in the kitchen where only hours earlier she had stood in Colin's arms while he kissed her. She yearned for what could never be, wished she had taken more of his loving to store in her memory when she was far from him.

She stared at the note she had written, feeling it was inadequate. Tears blurred her eyes, and she knew she should get up and go, but it was difficult to tear herself away. Finally she stood and propped the note in the middle of the kitchen table. Placing the pen on the table, she left the room.

Dressed in her new jeans and sweater, she pulled on one of Colin's old jackets and tucked Emily into her carrier. The suitcase was loaded into Colin's Jeep. She hated taking the Jeep, but there was no other way to get from his place without his knowledge. The extra key was tucked into her pocket. She paused in the kitchen for one last look around. Tears spilled over. She was going to miss Colin Whitefeather more than she would have guessed. It hurt to tell him goodbye. Her gaze fell on the note and she crossed the room, setting Emily in her seat on the kitchen table.

"I have to write one more thing to Colin," she said to Emily, who smacked her lips and gazed back unperturbed.

Katherine picked up the pen. A tear fell on the page and she brushed it away hastily, waving the note to dry the paper. She reread her note and then signed it.

"I'll love you always, Katherine." She pressed the paper to her heart. "I love you, Colin Whitefeather. I didn't think I would ever love again, and it won't do me any good because you can't love me back. Even if you could,

I wouldn't stay. I won't drag you into Sloan's path. But I love you.''

She opened her eyes, wiping at them swiftly. She bent over the table to add another note.

Thank you for making me able to love again.

She propped the note in the center of the table, turned off the alarm and picked up Emily. ''We better go like the wind, because if Colin finds us or sees us leaving, he'll interfere.''

She rushed to the Jeep and buckled Emily's seat into place, checking that Emily was fastened securely. Katherine opened the door, climbed behind the wheel and backed out, her gaze searching the land for signs of anyone, Colin, Sloan, Colin's men.

She hopped out and closed the garage door and swung the Jeep in a circle. Her hair was pinned up, with the most battered of Colin's hats on top. She prayed if Sloan's men were watching the place and saw her, they would think one of Colin's men was heading into town.

She drove at a normal speed although every nerve screamed to race away. Her gaze continually swept the land ahead, as well as the view in the mirror behind. At any moment she expected to see Colin come roaring up in the blue pickup.

Her skin prickled as she approached the highway. No car moved in behind her for the first twenty minutes and then one came into view, gaining on her. It was a green pickup with two men inside, and her pulse raced. When they tore on past her without a glance, she decided they had no connection to Sloan.

As she approached Stillwater, there was no suspicious black car behind her. She went through town, taking the highway east and then making a loop to turn onto the interstate to Oklahoma City. In heavier traffic it was impossible to tell whether she was being followed or not. The road was filled with black cars. The men could have changed to another car by now. As she neared the city, she noticed a black sedan close behind. When she signaled for the off-ramp, the car signaled and followed her.

Her pulse jumped and she drove swiftly across town, changing lanes suddenly, trying to follow a map as she drove, circling the city. In minutes the car was gone and Katherine pulled into a restaurant parking lot to study the map. She talked to Emily, who slept while they sped toward the airport.

As Katherine walked through the upper level of the airport, her skin prickled. At the ticket counter she looked around casually, but she couldn't spot any men focused on her. She went to her gate and found a nearby ladies' room where she settled in the anteroom to feed and change Emily. Over and over it ran through her mind that she was leaving Colin and the parting hurt. She almost expected to see him come charging through the airport after her, but common sense told her he would not.

When she boarded the plane, she looked at each passenger as he came on board. If anyone was following her, she couldn't tell.

As the plane lifted from the runway and she looked down at patches of pasture and plowed fields, she glanced at her watch. Ten minutes after four. When would Colin get back to the house? Stroking Emily's soft cheek, Katherine thought about her note. She did love Colin Whitefeather. It was hopeless, futile, impossible. They would never see each other again, although she knew she would write him. Would he ever come to California to see her? She doubted it, suspecting Colin would never risk his heart for anyone. The realization that she had fallen in love with him still amazed her.

She touched the smooth glass of the window as she looked at the Oklahoma landscape below, looking at the winding thread of the Cimarron River bed, the water almost as red as the banks. Fields were plowed in long, neat furrows and squares of winter wheat were bright green patches in the earth's blanket.

The view below vanished as all she saw was the mental image of Colin, standing in his kitchen, strong, full of vitality, laughing, with his white teeth a contrast to his dark skin. She loved him and he would never really know it. He would pay little attention to her note, except to know that she had gone. How had he won her love so swiftly?

At half past two Colin quit early. He hadn't gone back to eat breakfast and his stomach was churning with hunger. Even more urgent, he wanted to get home to see Katherine.

As he opened the back door, the dogs bounded into the kitchen. No tempting smells of Katherine's cooking met him, no cheery call came; Emily's cry didn't break the silence and instantly Colin became wary.

"Katherine!"

When he heard only the shuffling of the dogs, his hand went to his pistol. "Katherine!" he called again, but he didn't expect an answer this time. "Damn," he said, his alarm growing until he saw the folded square of white paper standing in the middle of the kitchen table. His heart thudded, and without picking up the note he knew she was gone.

He walked over to read the note. *I love you, Colin Whitefeather.* The words took his breath. He ran his thumb across it, momentarily distracted, forgetting the rest of her message. Had she written it casually? Katherine didn't strike him as the type of person to toss "I love you" around lightly. *I love you, Colin...* The words seemed to wrap around his heart and squeeze painfully.

He placed the note carefully on the table and sat down. She was gone. He would have to go to the city to pick up his Jeep. She had wanted to get on with her life and she was on her way to California now. He looked at the note again. No one had broken in and made her write it—she was ready to go and had chosen to leave without saying goodbye.

As he stood, he pushed his hat back on his head and unbuttoned his coat. He longed for her and for Emily. The house was too quiet. Both dogs were sitting, watching him. "Okay, fellas," he said. "The lady and our little girl are gone. We knew she was going." He leaned against the counter and closed his eyes. It hurt so badly. He had lost her and he didn't like the way he felt. Lobo nudged his knee and Colin opened his eyes to get the dog food.

"Yeah, yeah. You want to eat and to hell with missing the lady. You'll miss her tonight when you want your ears scratched or a yummy scrap from the table. I don't remember this house being so damned empty. Why don't you fellas learn to talk?"

Emily's bib lay on the kitchen counter and he picked it up, running his finger over the bright red trimming. He hurt and he missed Katherine and Emily. Crushing the bib in his hand, he pressed it against his heart as if he could hold a tiny part of them there. He tossed aside the bib and turned to take care of the dogs. With his jaw clenched until it hurt, Colin emptied dog food into two large bowls and ran fresh water into a bucket he set down in the garage.

"There, you greedy rascals. You're not giving me much sympathy. You'll be looking for her soon enough. You'll miss her, too."

Colin went inside and closed the back door. The house was silent and he swore as he crossed the room, got a beer from the fridge and looked at leftovers of food she had cooked. He went back to pick up her note. *I love you, Colin...*

With a sigh he tossed down the note. Even if she had stood in the kitchen and told him she loved him to his face, she would have wanted to go on to California and he would have let her go. He wasn't going to marry again. He couldn't offer her anything.

He moved to the window. Was he sure he didn't want to take another chance? The lady had fit into his life in an amazing way. Who said he couldn't change and love again? It wasn't written in stone, and he hadn't signed any contract promising he would never love again. He thought of all the times he had promised himself he wouldn't run such risks again, but Katherine had simply climbed into his life with the same swift ease she had climbed into his pickup. He missed her.

"Let her go," he told himself. "She knows what she wants and she's going for it. Let the lady go."

He had little choice. She had already gone. He didn't feel like eating. He crossed the room and switched on the answering machine. At first when the man's voice came on, Colin was thinking about Katherine and barely listening. And then he realized what he was hearing.

"Dammit!" He backed up the tape and turned it on to play it again.

I'm bringing you home. Don't fight me when I come for you. Don't bring trouble down on someone who is no part of our lives. You're going to cause innocent people to get hurt if you keep hiding behind them. Colin swore and slammed his fist against his palm. Sloan's call was why she had gone. Colin was certain she had fled to protect him. He swore again, listening to the rest of the tape, his temper soaring.

We can work out our differences. Dad and I hoped you would have a boy to carry on our name, but once again you disappointed me. I'll see you soon. Don't let others get hurt because of your foolishness.

The phone clicked and Colin strode to his room. He had been mistaken about her reasons for leaving. She hadn't gone because she wanted to get on with her life or was ready to tell him goodbye. She had fled because of Sloan's phone call.

Colin shivered. She could have gone right into a trap. The call was meant to flush her out. If only she had waited until he had come home, but he was certain why she hadn't.

He wanted to get his hands on Sloan Manchester. How he would like to encounter the man! Colin gathered money, his pistol, checking his closet to see which hat and coat she had taken so he would know what to look for. In minutes he was charging down the road in his blue pickup. Hunched over the wheel, his knuckles were white as he clutched the steering wheel. Had she made it to the airport? And which airport? Tulsa or Oklahoma City? The men were bound to be close behind her if they hadn't already picked her up. Would he be able to find her trail? Would he know if Sloan had caught her and picked her up? If he had, Katherine and Emily could be on their way back to New Orleans right now. Where was Sloan Manchester?

All the way to Stillwater he talked to reservation centers on his cellular phone, trying to decide which flight she would try to catch. At Stillwater he took a chance on Oklahoma City.

He found the Jeep in the airport parking lot at five minutes to four. It took him another ten minutes to find an attendant who remembered seeing a tall woman in a cowboy hat carrying an infant and a suitcase. In another five minutes he learned she had bought a ticket to San Francisco with a stopover in Dallas.

His heart jumped as he faced the pretty brunette who

was smiling at him with curiosity in her eyes. "I noticed her because she was tall and she was carrying a tiny, adorable baby."

"That's my wife," he lied, yet something about the statement sounded so damn right.

"Well, sir, I'm sorry. That plane—" she paused to glance at her watch. "It just took off a few minutes ago."

He swore. "Is there another flight?"

"I'll check." As she punched a keyboard and studied a screen she flicked her gaze to him. "You're not the only man asking about her. But the other man didn't say it was his wife. He said it was his sister."

Colin bit back the words that rose in his throat. Now Sloan knew her destination and she would be in as much danger in San Francisco as she had been in in Oklahoma.

"I'm sorry, sir. Our next flight leaves in two hours."

"Thanks." He was gone, running to a phone to call other airlines. After three frantic calls he found a flight and in minutes ran to the gate as they were closing the doors. He boarded another Dallas flight, which would land within twenty minutes of hers and thirty minutes before her flight was due to leave for California.

He shifted in the seat, looking at the passengers. She had made it onto the plane to Dallas. Had she been followed?

Sloan or his men knew Katherine was on the Dallas flight. They would probably pick her up in the Dallas airport and head to Louisiana. Colin moved restlessly, wanting to urge the plane forward. Impatiently, he stood and found a flight attendant. He pulled out his badge.

"Would it be possible to talk to the captain? Here's my problem...." He gave the barest details about a woman on the run from an obsessive ex-husband, telling her he needed to be in Dallas to find her and protect his fiancée.

He asked if it would be possible to shave any time off the trip.

The captain came back to talk to him and Colin flashed his badge and explained in more detail.

"We can't get you much extra time, but the weather is clear and we can maybe give you ten minutes."

"I'll be grateful forever."

The man nodded and Colin returned to his seat to glance at his watch.

The moment they landed he was up the aisle, the first to leave. As he passed the tall dark-haired captain, he nodded. "Thanks a million."

"Good luck."

Running down the jetway, Colin knew he would need it. With a mounting sense of frustration, he searched for airport security and the moment he found a uniformed man he flashed his badge. "I need to get to gate 28C as quickly as possible."

"C'mon. We'll talk as we go," the security guard said, flagging down a cart and climbing on, motioning to Colin to sit beside him.

Colin looked at his watch. Her flight had left Oklahoma City at ten past four and arrived in Dallas at ten past five. She had fifty minutes until takeoff to California. It was now thirty-five minutes past five. The plane to California would be boarding any minute now. Or Sloan could have already taken her with him and be heading to another flight or to a car.

The crowd in the terminal seemed to multiply before Colin's eyes. And the cart seemed to be moving in slow motion. He wanted to jump down and race through the airport, but he suspected the cart would get there faster and draw less attention.

And then as they approached the designated gate, he saw two burly men standing yards apart across the wide hall near a ladies' room. He almost rode past them without notice, but something about one of them registered and he remembered that snowy day when he had watched two men striding down the street after Katherine. He couldn't identify those men, yet instinct told him he was looking at them again. And if he was, Katherine must be hiding in the ladies' room.

He caught the arm of the security man. "The two guys—one in jeans, one in slacks. They're watching the ladies' room. Can you think of some pretext to get them both out of sight of that door long enough for me to get her away?"

Colin knew if he was wrong he was going to waste time and lose her completely, but he had survived in the past by hunches and gut instincts. Right now he felt Katherine was close at hand.

"The men aren't together. That will make it tougher."

"Think of something. Tell them they fit the description of two men who are wanted, and would they mind going with you to talk to your supervisor."

"Yeah. I better get a supervisor."

"Take him," Colin said, pointing toward a flight attendant who was in uniform.

"They won't go for it."

"They'll go for your badge. And I don't think they want to draw attention to themselves. Give me two minutes with them away from the door," Colin said, folding a twenty-dollar bill and holding out his hand.

The man looked at him and down at his hand while he considered. He sighed. "I won't promise anything."

"Thanks." Colin passed the twenty to the man and it vanished from sight as Colin stepped off the cart. He waited while the cart made a final stop and then reversed direction. The cart halted, the guard stepped off and talked to the flight attendant, then he turned and walked toward one of the men. The flight attendant sauntered down the hall and disappeared through a closed door marked for employees only.

Walking to a newspaper vending machine, Colin dropped coins in the slot and removed a paper. While he glanced at it, he kept his back to the men. When he turned around the two were arguing with the guard. In minutes they walked with him down the hall and through the same door where the flight attendant had gone.

Colin strode swiftly to the ladies' room and stepped inside without hesitation. "Katherine!" he shouted.

Nine

A woman washing her hands turned to look at him open-mouthed. His gaze swung around an anteroom where Katherine sat on a red vinyl sofa.

"C'mon," he snapped as he looked into Katherine's wide green eyes. And then she was moving. She gathered her things and rushed toward him. He reached out to take Emily, who was buckled into her carrier, her big blue eyes studying him solemnly.

As Katherine passed him and stepped into the hall, his gaze flicked over her, taking in his battered western hat, his old jacket, which hung below her waist and the few tantalizing inches of tight jeans that were snug over her trim bottom and her long legs. He followed her into the hallway.

"How did you get—"

"They're after you. C'mon."

Grabbing Katherine's bags, he glanced over his shoulder. "C'mon, Katherine. If I tell you to run, you run. They're here and they know you're here."

Colin turned one direction and she turned another. She caught his arm. "My plane to California is this way."

"They know where you're going. You won't be safe going to California now. C'mon," he said, tugging lightly on her arm.

Clamping her lips closed, there was only a moment's hesitation, and then she trotted to keep up with his long stride, her lower lip caught in her teeth.

"How'd you find me?"

"Pure luck and fast moves. I spotted them waiting for you outside the ladies' room."

"I saw them and ducked inside," she said breathlessly.

"If we can get out of here—" Colin's mind raced. He couldn't take time to go through the formalities of renting a car. Any minute now the men would spot them. He headed for the front of the airport.

Katherine raced at his side, her thoughts tumbling. *Colin was here!* She had thought she would never see him again, yet here he was, holding Emily, taking them home with him. Never had he looked more marvelous than when she had glanced up, hearing him yell her name. His black hat sat squarely on his head and he had a determined jut to his jaw. She glanced over her shoulder, half expecting to see the two men racing after them.

Lights were bright when they rushed outside. Cars were lined up, people unloading luggage, others placing suitcases into cars and vans. Taxis passed and shuttles slowed to park near the curb. A smell of diesel fuel permeated the air. Colin hesitated and then took her arm.

"See that bright red sports car? When we get to it, climb inside."

"Is that someone you know?" she asked, looking at a longhaired teenager behind the wheel. Music carried loudly from the car. The windows were down, the sunroof was open and the teen was thumping his hand on the steering wheel in time to the beat of the music. Colin rushed around to the driver's side while Katherine opened the door on the opposite side.

"Hey, man!"

"Payne County sheriff's department," Colin said, flashing his badge. "Move over. We need to use your car for just a few minutes."

"Hey! I don't know no Payne County—"

Colin waved the badge under his nose. "Move it or I call the local cops."

"Well, damn," he said, scooting to the passenger seat and turning to look at Katherine, who flashed him a brilliant smile.

"Thank you, so much. This is a matter of life and death."

"Sure, lady," he said, turning to look more fully at her. Colin passed Emily and the carrier to Katherine.

"Tell me when she's buckled in," he said. "I'll drive slow until then."

"Hey, you drive slow all the time. This is a new car, man."

"He'll be very careful," Katherine said, patting the teen on the shoulder.

The teen turned to Katherine. "My name's Ziggy."

"I'm Katherine and this is my daughter, Emily," she said, flashing another smile.

"Your old man?" Ziggy asked, jerking his head in Colin's direction as Colin glanced at him and then returned his attention to his driving.

"No, I'm divorced."

"No kidding!" Ziggy turned to Colin. "Hey, man, how long are you keeping my car? I'm picking up some people and I won't be there when they arrive."

"You'll be back in no time. Just want to get to a hotel."

"Emily is buckled in," Katherine said, looking out the rearview mirror.

Colin pressed the accelerator and they sped away from the airport, weaving through traffic. He stayed just above the speed limit and in ten minutes pulled up before the entrance to a tall hotel.

"Here we are. Thanks, kid. Help the lady out of the car."

"You bet!"

As Colin came around the car, Katherine was bent over, trying to unbuckle Emily's infant carrier. The jeans pulled tautly over her bottom and Ziggy was staring at her openmouthed. And Colin could see why. If the situation were different, he would like to stand and ogle her too, but he didn't want anyone else to do so.

He dangled the keys in front of the teen's face. "Here." Along with the keys Colin handed a twenty-dollar bill to him. "This will cover the gas I used. And forget you ever saw us."

"Yeah! Hey, sure," he said, his eyes widening. "Hey, thanks, man." He smiled at Katherine.

Colin took Emily and the carrier from Katherine. He picked up her suitcase and strode into the hotel. "I'll get us a rental car and we'll be on our way out of here. You watch for anyone following us."

Within fifteen minutes they were settled in a black sedan, heading north to Oklahoma.

Katherine tossed off the hat and his coat, straightening the red sweater she wore. It clung to her figure and Colin felt a tightening in his groin. Color had returned to her face and Colin wanted to pull to the side of the road and put his arms around her and reassure himself that she was really with him again.

"You came because you heard Sloan's message, didn't you?"

"Yes. I could imagine your panic."

"After I was airborne, I remembered his message was still on the machine. I should have erased it."

"When I heard it, I figured that's why you fled in such a rush."

"Colin, in the airport you didn't give me time to think, but going home with you isn't solving anything. Sloan will still come after me. The men searching for me will keep hunting me. I don't want you hurt."

"I'm not scared of Sloan. He has to be careful what he does to others. He's in the limelight, running for public office. He can't do anything too bad or it'll kill his political career."

Katherine looked at the dark countryside whipping past as they sped north on the interstate. Trees dressed in new leaves stretched dark branches toward the sky and the air held a promise of spring.

In spite of Colin's presence, she felt cold, a premonition of disaster making her shake. She turned back to look at Colin's profile, his slightly arched nose, his strong jaw, the prominent cheekbones. He had rugged features that went with his forceful personality. His hair was tied behind his head, the broad-brimmed black hat sitting squarely on his head.

"Sloan has a violent temper. After a certain point, he stops thinking. He's hurt people before—not just me. I told you about the time in college, but there have been other times he's hurt someone. His father always covered for him, until Sloan was wealthy and powerful enough to protect himself. He could easily hurt you in a moment of rage and then try to cover it up. If your body was found out on your land, no one would know. Or if your car crashed into a bridge some night—no one would know."

SARA ORWIG 143

"That kind of killing is premeditated—not someone losing it in a fit of rage."

She shrugged. "I'm warning you, Colin, he's capable of what I just said. To get to me, he'll hurt you if he has to."

"Okay, I'm warned. How many ex-cops has he tangled with?"

"None that I know about."

"I'll take my chances. Just tell me if you see him coming."

"I still have to go to California."

"They know you bought a plane ticket to San Francisco."

Colin glanced at her, his dark eyes momentarily holding her gaze. She closed her eyes, wondering whether she would ever be safe again. Every mile closer to Colin's ranch, took her closer to more problems.

"I'll go somewhere else. I won't tell you or anyone."

"If you're taking correspondence courses with LSU and you forward your address, you know he can easily find it."

"I won't contact the college until after the election. I want my degree. I need to have a livelihood to support Emily."

Colin glanced at her, remembering her note. *I love you, Colin...* How simple it would be to marry her. He could give her protection and provide for both of them. She would fill the void in his life, the aching, bitter loneliness. He glanced in the rearview mirror at Emily, who was sitting quietly, her blue eyes wide while she toyed with the ruffles of a blanket Katherine had tossed over her. The barriers in his heart came up. He wasn't going to open himself to that terrible kind of hurt again.

He clenched his jaw closed. It would be so easy. Only a few words to Katherine. He thought about the loss of

Dana and the hell he had gone through afterward. Never again. And this woman brought all kinds of trouble with her. So why was he taking her home with him? To seduce her or to protect her?

If only he could do something to get Sloan off her trail permanently, then he would know Katherine was safe and happy and he would forget this time in his life. He glanced again at Emily who was rubbing her cheek with the corner of her blanket. His harsh thoughts melted as he looked at the tiny baby who was being so quiet. She hadn't caused anyone trouble since she came into the world.

He shifted his gaze to the road. "I'll help you find some place to go. I have a friend in Arizona. You might go there for a time and then move on when it's safer."

"You're very good to us," Katherine said quietly, looking down at her fingers in her lap. She shifted in the seat to look out the window and they both became quiet. She was going back. She would have more time with Colin. She thought about the feeling of loss she had experienced while driving to the city and in the airport. She would have one more chance with Colin, a few more hours with him. An inner voice urged her to grab whatever happiness the moment gave her, to not hold back this time, because after this time there would be no other chance.

She studied his profile. She could ask him to love her, to know once what it was like to be loved by someone who cared beyond his own pleasure. And she knew Colin would care beyond himself. She knew this tough, strong man would give pleasure beyond what he took. This was a chance for that moment: did she want to take it?

The moon was large and white, spilling over the landscape with a silvery coldness. They ate at a drive-in in Oklahoma City and then headed toward Stillwater and his ranch.

"Shouldn't we pick up your Jeep at the airport?"

He shook his head. "Someone might be watching it. I'll send one of the men to get it. Someone's always going to the city for one reason or another."

She settled back in the seat and they rode in silence. As the miles whipped past she mulled over her choices, still unable to come to a conclusion.

When they entered the ranch house, Colin saw her note still lying on the kitchen table. He picked it up and tucked it into his pocket as he set Emily and her carrier on the kitchen table. She began to cry and he unbuckled her and picked her up. "I can't feed you, sweetie, but as soon as Mommy's fed you, I'll rock you."

Katherine set her bag on the floor and stood looking at him. "I'll take her."

He glanced around. "Katherine, I need to coach you in disguises," he said as his gaze slowly drifted over her from his battered gray Stetson to her toes. "You're as inconspicuous as a brass band. Anyone would notice a beautiful, tall woman in a cowboy hat and tight jeans."

"I thought when I left in your Jeep, if I wore your hat and coat, I might look like one of the men who work for you."

He handed Emily to her and gave her a faint smile. "Anyone who mistook you for a man needs more than glasses. They need a new brain."

Emily's lusty cries ended the conversation and Katherine left the room. He stepped outside into the moonlit night and surveyed his land. Where was Sloan Manchester now? How long until he knew she was back in Oklahoma?

Colin went inside and locked up, switching on the alarm at the gate. He pulled out the note and reread it, then carried it to his desk and placed it in a drawer. He made some calls, got out a cold beer and built a fire in the fireplace.

"You said you wanted to rock her. She hasn't gone to sleep," Katherine said.

She stood across the room with Emily in her arms. The red sweater was vivid, with Katherine's red hair and creamy skin. Her hair was looped and pinned on top of her head, but tendrils had escaped and were falling down and he wanted to pull it all down. He crossed the room to take Emily from her. Holding the tiny baby, he talked to her softly. Her wide blue eyes studied him intently while she sucked on her fist.

"I'm glad you're back with me. Do you know that? I missed my little girl."

Katherine looked up, wondering if he realized what he had said. She listened to him a moment longer. He seemed completely engrossed in Emily and had her rapt attention. Katherine quietly left the room to unpack, looking at the bedroom she had fled less than twenty-four hours earlier. She could hear the rumble of his voice as he talked to Emily, the creak of the floorboards when he rocked. She closed her eyes as pain twisted her heart. Why did she have to be tied to a man like Sloan?

She shook her head. It wouldn't matter if there had never been a man in her life. Colin was not going to love again. She suspected he had opened his heart more for Emily than for anyone else since the loss of his wife.

She showered and put fresh underclothes and the red sweater and jeans on again, feeling as if she had washed away the fears of the day. She remembered looking down the hall at the airport and seeing the two men staring at her, knowing they intended to take her back to Louisiana to Sloan. She could hardly believe her eyes when Colin stepped into the ladies' room, yet at the same time it seemed like the most natural thing in the world to have him appear. And the first reaction she had was to want to run and throw her arms around him.

She went to the front room, pausing a moment to look at him. He was seated near the fire, his profile to her as he rocked Emily, who had gone to sleep. He stroked the baby's head and then her cheek and Katherine felt another deep yearning, regretting that she could never have more of Colin than what she had right now.

She crossed the room and leaned down. "I'll put her in bed."

"I'll do it," he said, standing and carrying Emily to the cradle in the bedroom. Katherine followed him from the room, her gaze drifting down over him, remembering how it felt to be held against that long, powerful body. She watched while he tucked a tiny blanket over Emily.

"Sweet dreams, little girl," he whispered and turned around. He draped his arm across Katherine's shoulders and they went to the front room to sit on the floor near the fire.

She wrapped her arms around her knees. "You know Sloan will guess I'm back here with you."

"Sooner or later."

"Can they find out that I didn't board the plane?"

"Yes."

She turned to look at him. "I don't think I should stay here. I know you're not afraid, but I don't want you hurt. Your parents shouldn't have another heartache."

Colin reached out to draw a pin out of her hair and watch silky locks tumble down. He remembered that first night, when she had flinched if he stretched his hand toward her. Her green eyes widened as she watched him and he gazed at her, remembering, wanting her. He ached to kiss and hold her, and for weeks now he had been banking the fires he felt. He removed another pin and another, until her hair cascaded over her shoulders.

"I missed you," he said gruffly, placing his hands on both sides of her face. Her bones felt delicate, her skin soft. The hungry look in her green eyes made his pulse jump. She leaned forward, her gaze shifting to his mouth, and his pulse jumped again.

Katherine twined her arms around his neck. Desire streaked in her, a heat that burned low in her body and then spread, making her limbs feel heavy. She wanted this man's love. If only once, she wanted a man's love that was true and honest. He didn't have to give her promises, but he could give her memories. More than she had now. Good memories, to block out the pain and heartache of the past.

All the long hours driving to the city and waiting in the airport, she had thought about what she had let slip past. She wanted Colin's strong arms around her, wanted his hands on her, she wanted to know his body, discover him fully. Their lovemaking could hold no permanence. She understood that. He couldn't give her tomorrow, yet he could give her tonight.

They could have a night of love, or two nights or three, before they had to say good-bye. Something she could treasure, loving that would make her feel like a desirable woman again. And maybe for a few nights she could give him the illusion of completeness. Maybe she could ease the sting of his loss and he would see that someday he could open his heart again completely.

She looked into his dark eyes, wanting him, willing to risk the heartache of loving and telling him goodbye. Her heart was lost to him anyway, whether she spent the night in his arms or alone in his bed. He studied her and she gazed back and then looked again at his mouth, which was sensual and masculine with his sculpted lips, his slightly thick lower lip. She lowered her head and placed her mouth on his deliberately.

He groaned, his arm going around her waist to crush her against his chest. His mouth moved on hers, opening hers wider, his tongue dancing over hers. He shifted her, pulling her into his lap to cradle her head against his shoulder as he bent one knee. Minutes later, in a fluid motion he stood and pulled her up into his arms to kiss her hard, a demanding kiss with his tongue going deep into her mouth, a lightning kiss that awakened fires in her.

This was no delicate, careful kiss such as he had given her before, trying to ease past her fear. His kiss now was as stormy as the roll of thunder. Tremors of response rocked her. Heat streamed into every niche and fiber of her body, kindling an urgency. She wanted this man's love and she wanted to love him in return. And the realization of the depths of her need shocked her.

She melted against him, thrusting her hips against his body, feeling his hard shaft, which was clear evidence of what he wanted. And she knew she had made the right decision. She was where she belonged and it would have been another tragic loss if she had caught her plane to California and missed Colin's loving. She belonged in his arms and she needed his kisses. And she would not think beyond the present. There was now, and that was all she needed to know.

"Katherine," he whispered in a raspy voice that was like sandpaper running over her nerves. "I've waited so long."

Her heart pounded and she felt cherished, desired. The feelings made her arch her back and wiggle against him. She had known he wanted her, but it warmed her to hear him say it.

"If I get too rough..." he whispered, his tongue flicking into her ear and then touching her throat. He took tiny bites of her flesh below her ear. "Stop me. One word. I promised you I'd never hurt you and I don't want to frighten you, either."

"You'll never get too rough," she answered, clinging to him, kissing him as passionately as he kissed her. "And

I'll never be afraid of you," she whispered, flicking her tongue over his lips. She ground her hips against him.

With a growl deep in his throat, he caught her up more tightly against his body, his hand sliding down over the small of her back, cupping her bottom to pull her up against him.

She kissed him hard, her tongue playing over his, exploring his mouth, touching his tongue. His hand slipped beneath her sweater, freeing her bra and pushing it away. He caught the hem of her sweater and tugged it over her head, flinging it aside while he gazed at her with a heavy-lidded look filled with desire.

Another tremor ran through her and she arched closer against him, as his hands played over her as lightly as the wind. His hands cupped the weight of her breasts, his thumbs flicking over her nipples. Sensations rocked her and she clung to his arms, which felt as solid as the branches of a tree except that his flesh was warm and smooth to touch. This lean, powerful man, with his strength and fierce ways, shook as he kissed and touched her.

The realization of the effect she was having on him astounded her. She tugged his shirt out of his jeans and pulled it over his head. Drawing a deep breath, she gazed at his broad chest. She trailed her hands over him, hearing his sharp intake of breath and then his groan.

"I can't believe I can have this effect on you," she whispered, kissing the corner of his mouth.

"You can't begin to guess what you do to me," he said gruffly. "I'm hot. I'm hard. I can barely speak. I've got the shakes. All because of you, Kat. My defenses are gone."

She looked into dark eyes that echoed what he had just admitted to her and the knowledge of his response to her was overwhelming.

"I didn't know I could do anything like this."

"You do all that and a lot more that I can't put into words," he said in a husky voice.

Colin held her tightly, his arm around her waist while he kissed her hard. He ached to carry her to bed and sink himself into her soft body, but he wanted to wait, to pleasure her, to give her memories and create ones for himself. They were grabbing a moment in time, and it would be a bright bubble that would burst all too soon and be gone forever.

He bent his head, taking her breast in his mouth, his tongue flicking over the tiny bud that was taut with arousal. And then he unbuttoned her jeans and pushed them away, kneeling to tug off her boots. Her hands wound in his hair while he trailed kisses over her stomach and hooked his fingers into her lacy pink panties and pulled them down.

Her skin was silken, warm beneath his tongue, her body vibrant and responsive to his every caress. He shook, feeling constrained by his jeans, aching to possess her, yet determined to drive her over a brink where dark memories of the past couldn't rise up to haunt her. He wanted to banish all her past, to let her know how good it could be between a man and woman who loved each other.

The knowledge slammed into him as if he had stepped off the edge of a twenty-story building. They loved each other. He denied it instantly. He was not going to give his heart away. This beautiful, gutsy woman had gotten beyond so many of his defenses, but she was not getting past the final defense. And he knew she didn't want to, that she had already mapped out a future for herself and Emily and it did not include him. Just a night of loving, but that was more than he had dreamed he would have.

He trailed kisses along her throat. Right now he wanted to give to her until she was so lost to passion she forgot

every bad moment in her past. His mouth covered hers
while his hand caressed her inner thighs and moved to the
moist warmth between her legs. She was ready for him,
so eager and ready, yet he wanted her shaking with need.

Her fingers fumbled on the buttons of his jeans until she
gasped and gripped his arms while her hips moved con-
vulsively. He swung her into his arms and carried her to
bed, lowering her and then trailing kisses across her belly.

His kisses were possessive, his hands and tongue playing over her as if he were claiming her inch by inch. And
with a primitive surge of joy, she knew that hereafter when
she thought of lovemaking, she would remember this night
and all before it would fade to a dim nightmare.

Colin's head lowered at the juncture of her thighs, his
tongue sending fiery streaks of pleasure through her as her
body arched beneath his kisses.

Thought spun away and she cried out his name, stroking
his shoulders, writhing with a need as he took her to a
brink.

"Colin!"

"That's it, Kat. Want me. Let me love you."

With a cry she surged up off the bed, tugging his arm
as he stood facing her. Her hands tore at the remaining
buttons on his jeans and she pushed them away. She
caught her fingers in the tight band of his briefs and pushed
them down and rested her hands on his hips. He was mag-
nificent and she wanted to drink in the sight of him. Broad
shouldered, muscular, Colin was handsome. His body was
ready for her, his male shaft thick and erect and she
reached out to close her fingers around him and then stroke
him.

He gasped and placed his hands on her hips while she
knelt to take him in her mouth, stroking him with her
tongue, returning the tormenting ecstasy he had given her.

She heard his groan of pleasure and need, felt his big

hands tangling in her hair, saw his body shake. Her hand slid between his legs, cupping him, stroking him so lightly, discovering his male body and loving it.

Suddenly he pulled her to her feet, his dark eyes driving into her with a stunning look so filled with need it took her breath.

Never in her life had a man looked at her with the blazing yearning that was unmistakable in Colin's gaze. He hauled her against his chest to kiss her in wild possession, and then they moved together. He swung her onto the bed and opened the drawer of a bedside table. "I've got protection."

As he knelt between her legs, she caught his hands and tossed down the small packet. "Let me take some chances."

"Katherine—"

"I know what I want," she said, her huge green eyes enveloping him.

"Next time, love," he said, leaning down to retrieve the packet and opening it. "I can't argue or discuss anything. You're beautiful!" he said, his gaze raking over her.

Her fingers closed around him. She guided him as he leaned down, and then she closed her eyes. His shaft was big and she was tight, and when he entered her sensations exploded in her. Her hips moved while she wrapped her long legs around him and clenched her body. They were one in body and in heart!

Joy soared in her along with passion. She held him close, moving with him, the crashing need building until she was caught on a tide that was beyond her control.

"Colin, oh, my love—"

His arms tightened around her as he moved with her. She was hot and tight, her long legs locked around him. Dimly, he heard her cries and he felt complete. For the first time in so long, he felt whole. His aching loss vanished. He had Katherine in his arms, her softness enveloping him, her fire consuming him. His pulse thundered while his body moved frantically, claiming her, taking her and giving her passion in return.

"Kat, love." He ground out the words as sweat beaded his body.

Katherine dimly heard him say her name, heard the endearment. And then her body tightened, the intense sensations drowning out all sounds as she was carried up and over a brink, spasms of pleasure racking her while she felt his body shudder with his release.

They lay in each other's arms, satiated, drenched, immobile. Pounding heartbeats returned to normal. He shifted to kiss her throat, trailing kisses to the corner of her mouth. She turned her head.

She felt boneless, incapable of moving, warm and loved. His loving had been perfection. His tenderness now was marvelous. She traced her finger along his firm jaw, feeling the hard bone, moving her fingertip over the point of his cheekbone. He turned his head, caught her finger between his teeth lightly, holding her for a moment before he released her. "Kat. How I've wanted you!"

She snuggled closer in his arms, feeling him tighten his grasp.

"Colin, you've given me so much." She turned her head, burrowing against his chest.

"Not tears?" he asked, worrying about her.

"No," she said, looking up and smiling. "Just pure one-hundred-percent joy."

"Me, too, lady. My tall redheaded lady. Thank heavens you climbed into my pickup."

"Thank heavens you offered!"

He held her close, their legs entwined while he thought about the marvel of Katherine and Emily in his life. "Stay here and let him come after you."

Her heart jumped. For one brief, shining moment she wondered if Colin meant he wanted her to stay forever. And in those few seconds she actually considered the possibility. But reality set in. She would not divert Sloan's wrath on him. Colin would willingly tangle with Sloan, but one of them would come away hurt, if not both, and she didn't want to risk it being Colin.

"If I knew he wouldn't bother you, I wouldn't worry as much when you're far away," Colin said.

His words brought back the last vestige of reality. She knew if the barriers had gone down around his heart in the past hour, they were back up now. He wasn't ready to let go and love anymore than she was ready to run risks with his life.

She stroked his shoulder, looking at his smooth, dark skin, tracing her finger down to his flat nipple, running her hands over the taut pectoral muscles.

"It's now, Colin. Forget tomorrow for a little while."

He turned to kiss her gently. "You're right. Now tell me, why no protection?"

She held him fiercely. "Don't go through life always thinking everything out, Colin. Your heart will grow rusty. I wanted you and if I take a part of you away with me, that might be good and right, too."

He tilted her head up to gaze into her eyes. "You're a wonderful woman and you're caught up in passion now, which has clouded your reason. You'll go to California and have a new life and someone will come along who will adore you. And you'll forget about life before him."

Katherine stared at him, feeling mildly annoyed at his decisions about her life. "Will I now? Well, I just can't wait to meet him. I'll write you about him, Colin, and how wonderful he is and where he takes me and how he makes love to me."

With a growl, Colin rolled her over on her back and slid above her, his dark eyes fiery. "Stop it!"

"You started it," she shot back. "What difference does it make to you? You're the one who—"

He kissed her hard, silencing her, damning himself for his stupid words. He didn't want to think about her in someone else's arms, wearing someone else's ring. He kissed her hard and in seconds passion drove thought from his mind as he held her tightly and entered her again.

The next time she lay in his arms, he avoided any mention of future or past. And they loved again until they fell into an exhausted sleep.

In the first rays of dawn, Katherine dreamed of his strong arms, his kisses that made her ache and tremble. She stirred and woke as his tongue was a flame across her belly. It hadn't been a dream, she thought, while she wound her fingers in his hair and gave herself over languidly to his loving.

Later, in the bright morning sunlight with mockingbirds whistling loudly enough to be heard through closed windows, she woke to discover she was alone in Colin's bed. She saw a note propped on the table and picked it up.

"Work beckons, although I think my legs may be too weak to hold me up. Emily, perfect child that she is, is still sleeping. I will come home for dinner. Noon dinner. I can't stay away any longer. Mom called—word travels fast in the hinterland—she wants to come *help*. Translation—she can't wait to get her hands on Emily again. Hope you don't mind. I told her to come over. She may be here when you wake."

Startled, Katherine looked at her nude body and glanced around, blushing furiously as she spotted bits of their clothing strewn around the room. She climbed out of bed, hurried to shower and then went to look for Emily.

Nadine Whitefeather sat rocking and talking to Emily.

She looked up and smiled as Katherine entered the room. "Good morning. I'm so glad you're back. I hope Colin told you that I might be over this morning. He asked me if I wanted to come."

"It's nice to have you," Katherine said, blushing furiously as she picked up her sweater and bra, which Colin had probably never given a thought to this morning. She knew Nadine had to have tiptoed into Colin's bedroom to get Emily. "We're back for a few days and then I should go." Katherine debated a moment and then sat down facing Emily and Nadine Whitefeather. "Has Colin told you about my ex-husband?"

Nadine shook her head. Emily stirred and began to cry, so Katherine took her.

"You can sit here," Nadine said, standing and letting Katherine have the rocker. "I just changed her a few minutes ago."

"I'm sure she's hungry," Katherine said, blushing again as she remembered Colin's mouth at her breast only hours before. As she fed Emily and rocked, she told Nadine more details about her life with Sloan and why she was running away.

"You'll work it out," Nadine said when she finished. "I just hope my stubborn son comes to his senses in time. He was hurt badly when he lost Dana. Men like Colin don't love easily, but when they love it's with the whole heart."

Katherine closed her eyes and rocked. "I'm not the woman for him to love." She opened her eyes to find Nadine watching her with the same dark eyes that Colin had. "I can only bring him danger and trouble."

"You two will work it out, except Colin can be a stubborn man. When you go, will you keep in touch? Will you send me a picture of Emily occasionally?"

"Of course," Katherine said, knowing she was going to miss Colin's mother and her steady, quiet warmth.

An hour before his mother left, Colin returned home. With a slam of the back door and the scrape of his boots, he brought a draft of cold air as he swung Katherine up in his arms and hugged her, kissing her hard. He was cold, his jaw bristly. He was male, strong, and holding her up in his arms he made her feel small and delicate, something she had rarely felt in her life until she met him.

"I feel as if I have been away from you for years instead of hours!" he grumbled.

"Good. I'm glad you missed me," she said softly, "because I missed you."

"Are we alone?"

"No."

He made a face and set her on the floor. He hung up his hat and coat and draped his arm across her shoulders. "Let's go find Mom and the wee one."

They fell into an easy pattern of loving and living and she knew it was an idyll that could not last, yet she took each hour with him as a magic treasure that she could hold forever in memory.

On Tuesday, the last week of April, she kept her doctor's appointment, got a prescription for birth control pills and went home to a night of loving in Colin's arms. Wednesday and Thursday Nadine came each morning to help with Emily and Katherine gladly relinquished the baby to Nadine's loving care, knowing that soon she would have to take Emily away and Nadine wouldn't see her again.

Thursday afternoon the phone rang. Katherine paused beside the machine, knowing Nadine was bathing Emily. When the tone beeped for a message, she heard Sloan's voice.

Ten

"Katherine? I want to talk to you."

Reluctantly, knowing that an eventual confrontation with Sloan would come, she picked up the phone. "I'm not going back to Louisiana."

"Can I at least come out and talk to you? Please. I'll come alone—no pressure, just give me a few minutes to discuss my campaign with you. If you're not coming back, at least let me have a statement for the public and maybe a campaign picture. Is that too much to ask?"

She stared out the window wanting to tell him no, knowing the cold fear that curled in the pit of her stomach was clouding her thinking. Yet from past experience, she was well aware Sloan could be deceptive. "Sorry, Sloan, no. I'm not letting you near Emily."

"Katherine, please. I'm asking nicely. I'll come alone. Talk to me and save that man you love some trouble."

"I thought so. You're back to threats," she said fiercely, her fear for Colin growing.

"And the warnings aren't idle. He works on a ranch. Do you know how vulnerable he is? Right now, someone has him in a rifle sight. He's in a pickup. Do you know how easy it would be to pick him off? Do you know how long it would take for someone to discover his body?"

Katherine gripped the phone until her knuckles hurt. "You're lying! You're trying to frighten me."

"You should know I carry out my threats," he said in a tone of voice that meant his rage was growing. She trembled, looking out the window, thinking about Colin and knowing she should have gone days ago. She should have packed and slipped away and never looked back. If she had, Colin would be safe.

"If I see you, you have to leave him alone."

"Of course. I have no interest in Colin Whitefeather."

It chilled her to hear Sloan call him by name. She wondered how much Sloan knew about Colin and his daily routines. "All right. Come out to the house. There's an alarm at the gate—"

"Turn it off."

"I don't know how."

"Then break the damn thing. Don't have cops coming out after me. I'll kill him, Katherine, if he gets in my way. Go turn off the alarm now and let me in. I'll be gone in ten minutes. I want a picture of you and a statement. Give me that much." The phone clicked and her mind raced.

Take Emily and your gun and go to the bunkhouse. She could remember Colin's instructions. But that was before Sloan had threatened him. If she ran, he might take out his rage on Colin. But she could get Nadine and Emily out of harm's way. She walked to the alarm box on the wall and stared at the buttons. She reached out to push the switch to *off*. With a glance at the clock, she rushed to the bathroom as Nadine was drying Emily. Nadine was laugh-

ing and cooing at Emily. When she glanced at Katherine,
her smile faded.

"What's wrong?"

"My ex-husband is coming. He wants to talk to me."

"I'll put a call in for Will. Colin has his pager and I
can get him—"

"No!" Katherine bit her lip, lowering her voice. "I'll
be all right. Sloan just wants a statement from me for the
election. And he won't try to take me away without Emily.
Will you take her to the bunkhouse? That way, he can't
get both of us."

"Are you sure you don't want help?"

"If I need help, I have a gun and I'll fire it. Or I'll call
the bunkhouse. Either way, if I signal I need someone, then
you page Colin. But not until then," she said urgently,
clasping Nadine's arm. "I don't want Colin hurt. Please,
don't do anything unless I call. And if you see Colin coming to the house, stop him."

"He won't be here this time of day. Are you certain
you want to see Sloan, Katherine?"

"Yes. Let's get Emily bundled up and you two go before Sloan gets here. He could have been close when he
called."

She left the room to get her purse, checking to make
certain her pistol was inside. She placed the purse on the
kitchen counter.

In minutes she stood in the doorway and watched Nadine with Emily in her arms. They rushed across the yard,
headed past the barn to the bunkhouse and then disappeared inside. Grimly, Katherine turned to gaze down the
road. She looked at herself, knowing Sloan would disap-
prove. She wore jeans and one of Colin's chambray shirts,
the sleeves rolled high. Her hair was in a long braid down
her back. Sloan liked her dressed, perfumed and looking

her best, whereas Colin had never seen her in a dress, nor did he seem to care.

Spring had brought its touches of renewal to the land and the fields were green with new leaves on the trees. Each day as she looked out at the land she felt a sense of hope, but now the sound of Sloan's voice had brought back the chill of foreboding.

She saw the car in the distance before she heard the motor. As the black sedan drew close, she became more nervous. Had she made a mistake sending Nadine away? Should she have paged Colin? In spite of her fear of Sloan, Katherine knew she did not want Colin involved.

Sloan drove to the back door, parked and climbed out to smile at her. Wind ruffled his blond hair. He wore a leather bomber jacket, charcoal slacks and brown leather gloves. He looked as handsome as a movie star with his square jaw, wide blue eyes and perfect features. And all she could feel was a chilling fear and dislike. How had she ever thought she was in love with him? He smiled, revealing even white teeth. She knew women turned to stare at him in public places and she knew women called him often. Why had he ever wanted her? She had often wondered that and she remembered asking him once when they were dating. He had looked her over with smug assessment.

"You were pretty, alluring, a challenge. My teammate, Zach Hayes wanted you. I wanted to take you away from Zach."

"I never dated Zach more than two times."

"That was because I stepped in."

Now Katherine watched Sloan approach, and knew that he would want her if he thought Colin Whitefeather wanted her.

"May I come in?"

She stepped aside and he entered the kitchen, looking

around him. "This is rustic. Really roughing it, aren't you? Enjoying a primitive way of living?"

"It's nice," she replied, closing the door and moving away from him, trying to put the distance of the entire kitchen between them.

"Yeah. I thought you'd be holding our daughter."

"She's not here."

His eyes narrowed. "Leave it to you to have a girl. I know it's supposed to be determined by my genes. I wanted a son and heir."

"What did you want to discuss? What kind of statement do you want, Sloan?"

"I want you to come home with me."

"Then you lied about wanting a statement. I won't go back to Louisiana."

"You might if you'll think about what I'm offering. If you come back, Katherine, I will set up a trust for our daughter that will take care of her every need for the rest of her life. Surely you can't deny that."

"Yes, I can. It wouldn't be worth it. I couldn't trust you to keep from abusing her."

"You're not really thinking about it. After I've gone, you think it over. I can give her everything. As a single mother, you can give her very little. You don't have an education."

"I'm getting one."

"Come back," he coaxed softly. "Katherine, I made terrible mistakes and I know it now. I've missed you. I swear, I will never hit you again. I promise on my life," he said vehemently. "You can have your own apartment. I will give you anything you want."

"I don't believe you. I've heard promises before," she said, knowing she was goading him into anger by not co-operating with him—and also knowing she was not going back. Never would she give him a chance to hurt Emily.

"All right. If nothing else, please make two public appearances with me, get some pictures taken and then you can go. If I get elected, then I can tell the public we've parted. By the time the next election rolls around, they won't care. I know how to win people over—I won you, didn't I?"

"Unfortunately, yes. I'm not going back with you and I won't let you near Emily."

"Please, I'm begging. I'll put it in writing. I'll do anything. I'm sorry for all the times I hurt you. Give us a chance to be a family—"

"You ruined those chances, Sloan. And you've made promises before and broken them. The answer is no."

His blue eyes blazed and his jaw set in a familiar line. "You're in love with the cop, aren't you?"

"Keep him out of this. I'm leaving here and I won't see him again." She edged toward the counter.

"You're lying."

Knowing his anger was growing, she moved back a step, reaching for her purse and her gun. His gaze dropped to her purse and then back to look her in the eye.

"I'm going to fight you for custody of her. You're not able to provide for her like I can. And you can't prove anything. My men have checked records and destroyed records. I have nothing to fear from you."

"I know you don't have anything to fear from me. Just leave me alone. Sloan, the divorce is a matter of public record. I'm amazed the reporters haven't stumbled across that before now."

"I've announced our reconciliation. If I can produce you soon, they'll believe me. I want you at my side," he said stubbornly, his voice rising as his control slipped. "It looks better."

"You're going to bring trouble on yourself by being so

damned unreasonable! Just tell them we're divorced and get on with your life."

"And let them poke and pry into why we separated—no!" he shouted. Immediately he clamped his jaw closed and stared at her and she knew he was slipping beyond the edge of control. In seconds she would have to deal with him physically, something she had never been able to do successfully because of his strength.

"All I'm asking is two public appearances. Why is that so impossible?" he persisted.

"Because it won't stop there. If I went back with you, I would be at your mercy again."

"Come back on your own. I'll leave you money for a plane ticket."

"No, Sloan. I won't do it."

He moved toward her and her heart raced. She opened her purse and as she reached for the gun, he lunged across the kitchen, tackling her and smashing her against the counter.

When her fingers closed on the grip of the pistol, his hand wrapped around hers. They struggled, and then he slammed her arm down on the counter.

As pain shot up her arm, she cried out. He yanked the gun away from her. She clutched her arm, wondering if he had broken it. Pain burned into her fingers and up to her elbow.

He jerked her around, sliding his arm around her waist to push her in front of him. "Damn you for pulling a gun on me!"

"I should have years ago."

"Don't fight me or Emily will lose her mother, and then I'll have her for certain."

"Not if you're wanted for murder."

"It's your gun with your prints on it. I still have on

gloves. Go with me, Katherine or I'll knock you uncon-
scious and take you."

She wondered if he was going to take her without Emily—something she hadn't believed he would do, but he
gave no indication of wanting to find the baby.

He hauled her up against him, twisting her arm behind
her until she cried out. "Now, Katherine, let's get Emily."

"We can't. She's at Colin's mother's house on the
neighboring ranch. And his father is home with them,"
she lied, knowing no one was home at his parents' house.

"All right, we'll just go. They'll think you ran off and
left her."

"Colin will know you came after me," she said.

"So let him follow us. He can't do anything to stop me.
He'll never find you."

"Stop and think, Sloan! You're going to be sorry." She
realized he had slipped over an edge. He had lost control
and was acting on his emotions now instead of reason. And
she knew he was at his most dangerous.

They went outside where he shoved her into the waiting
car, pushing her down on the seat and sliding in beside
her. Turning, he tossed her gun into the bushes and then
climbed into the car. "Buckle up. I don't want you jumping out."

She grabbed the door handle and Sloan hit her squarely
on the jaw. Light exploded along with pain and Katherine
fell back against the seat as he yanked the seat belt around
her and buckled it. "Try that again and I'll hit you
harder."

"This is kidnapping, Sloan. It'll catch up with you,"
she said, rubbing her aching jaw.

Starting the motor, he picked up a cellular phone with
the other hand and punched numbers. "The baby is on the
neighboring ranch with the guy's mother. The father's
home, too. Get Emily."

"Sloan—"

"You'll be glad to see her." He began to drive. "Two public appearances where you give me support, and I'll get you a plane ticket back here. That shouldn't be so unreasonable."

"You'll face criminal charges if Colin's parents get hurt," she said. "These are the kind of people who will fight to protect a tiny baby."

"Let them fight. It'll be easy to get a baby and get away."

She was silent, looking across the fields. "How did you know I was in love with him?"

"A guess. You've been here a long time."

"I'm not going to make those appearances."

"Yes, you will," he said. "Think about Emily and what a lot of money can do for her."

"You can't get away with this. You're not thinking—"

He slapped her with the back of his hand, snapping her head around.

"I'll get what I want. When we're in Louisiana and you have your baby with you, you'll do what I want. And if you give me a chance, I can be a good husband."

"Is this proof?"

He began to swear in a steady stream and as soon as she realized it wasn't directed at her, she followed his gaze. He was looking into the rearview mirror. She twisted in the seat to see the cloud of dust and the blue pickup gaining on them. Her blood ran cold as she watched Colin closing the distance between them. Sloan reached beneath the seat, and she guessed he was going for a gun.

"Don't shoot him. You can never get away with murder."

"I'm not going to shoot him," he said, pulling out a tire iron. "I'm going to beat the bastard to a pulp and then I'm taking you home."

"Sloan, let me go. He won't do anything if you let me go."

"I can't wait to get my hands on him," Sloan said in a deadly tone that made her tremble. His face was deep red and she knew from past times that he was in a mindless rage.

"Hang on," he snapped and slammed on the brakes, throwing the car into reverse to smash into the pickup. She was flung forward, the seat belt holding her. Her forehead hit the windshield, but then she was yanked back by the belt. Momentarily stunned, she rubbed her head. When she looked around, Sloan was out of the car, racing back as Colin shook his head.

Sloan yanked open the pickup door. She saw Colin raise a gun, heard the blast, but then he was out, wrestling with Sloan. The gun flew from his hand. Sloan swung the tire iron and Colin ducked as it smashed a window. Colin lunged at Sloan and both men went down.

Shaking, terrified of the damage Sloan could do with the tire iron, she yanked up the cellular phone and punched 911. When a voice answered, Katherine gripped the phone tightly. "Help. Sloan Manchester is trying to kidnap me. We're on the Colin Whitefeather ranch and he's attacked Colin. Please get help here."

"At the Whitefeather ranch north of town?"

"Please hurry."

"Yes, ma'am. We already have a unit on the way," came a steady voice.

She turned to look at the two men. Horrified, she watched as they battled. Both had thrown off their jackets. Colin's long black hair swung free and she could see his bloody mouth and cheek.

Sloan kicked Colin, who fell back against the pickup. Then Sloan ran at him, trying to gouge his eyes. Colin twisted away, slamming his fist into Sloan. Colin lunged at Sloan and both went down, Colin grabbing Sloan's head to slam it against the ground.

Sloan broke free, smashing his fist against Colin's jaw and sending him sprawling. Sloan scrambled up to try to stomp on Colin's throat.

Katherine gasped as Colin caught Sloan's foot and yanked him off balance and they tumbled together again. In seconds they were back on their feet, slugging each other until Colin ran at Sloan, grabbing him low and slamming him into the pickup. He threw a punch that caught Sloan squarely on the jaw and then he gave him a swift chop with the side of his hand that dropped Sloan to the ground.

She scrambled out as a chopper spun overhead and set down near them. The dried grass flattened out as the blades slowed and two armed men jumped out.

She reached Colin, who caught her in his arms. "Are you all right?" he asked.

"Yes," she said, holding him. "You're hurt," she said, hurting herself as she looked at his bloody face and torn clothing.

"Mom paged me."

"Looks like you didn't need us after all," Abe Swenson said.

She felt Colin's weight sag against her and he crumpled on the ground. "Colin!"

She knelt beside him while the sheriff bent down to feel for a pulse. "He's all right," Abe said. "His pulse is strong. Abe Swenson," he said, holding out a hand.

"I'm Katherine Manchester."

"You called 911."

"Yes. That's my ex-husband, Sloan Manchester," she said, noticing two men hauling Sloan to his feet. Colin groaned and rolled over on his back, opening his eyes.

"Okay?" Abe asked him.

"Yeah."

"I figured you were," Abe said. "We'll need some statements, but we can get them later today. Want to come to the office with us or drive in later?"

"Drive in," Colin answered.

"He tried to take you forcefully?" Abe asked Katherine.

"Yes. He hit me and he fought with Colin."

"Will you be willing to testify against him?"

"Yes," she said quietly, looking beyond him at Sloan, who stood staring at her through puffy eyes. His face was as bloody as Colin's, he stood holding one arm with the other hand and she wondered if he had a broken arm.

"Can you take care of this guy?"

"Yes," she answered, her gaze returning to Colin while she searched through the pocket of her jeans for a hand-kerchief, handing it to him. He placed it against his bloody cheek and winced as he sat up and groaned.

"Maybe you should take him by emergency on your way into town and get his ribs looked at," Abe said, standing. "We'll take Manchester to town."

"Thanks, Abe," Colin said. "Thanks for getting here quickly."

"But not too quickly, right? You probably enjoyed the fracas." Abe smiled and left. Katherine knelt beside Colin.

"Can you stand if I help you?"

"Yes." He came to his feet with a grunt. "I'm okay," he said, but he was weaving as if he would collapse again.

"I'll drive back and tell Nadine the police have been here and then I'm taking you to the hospital."

"I don't need to go to the hospital."

"Sure," she said dryly, steadying him as they walked to the car. She noticed they were assisting Sloan who was limping badly, hobbling as he held one foot off the ground.

She helped Colin into the passenger side of the car and

she slid behind the wheel, turning to drive back to the ranch house. Nadine came outside to meet them.

"I'm taking Colin to the hospital. The police have Sloan."

"Thank goodness! Call me from the hospital."

"This is foolishness," he grumbled, laying his head back against the seat and closing his eyes.

Katherine turned to drive toward town. The chopper was already out of sight.

"That ends it," Colin said. "Sloan can't cover this one up. I'm pressing charges. His political career is over."

For the first time, Katherine realized she was free. She glanced at the man beside her. Sloan no longer was a threat or stood between them. Emotions warred inside her: relief that Sloan would no longer be a threat and that he could not take Emily from her. At the same time, Colin rode in silence, and with each minute that ticked past she knew he had not opened his heart. The barricades were still up and he would kiss her and Emily goodbye and send them on their way to California now. A deep ache came. The pain was different from the hurts she had experienced before, it was soul deep and she suspected it was going to last a very long time.

They rode in silence and she reminded herself that all along she had known she would only have a brief time with him and then it would be over. She had never expected more, but she had started hoping for more. She glanced at him again. His cheek and temple were bloody, his mouth cut, his dark hair was a tangle. She remembered the fight, thinking he had looked every bit the fierce warrior.

"Do you hurt?" he asked her.

"I'm all right."

"Turn around here and let me see."

She looked at the empty stretch of road and glanced at him, then returned her attention to her driving.

"I'd like to hit him again."

"You did enough. Both of you did," she said shivering, remembering their dreadful fighting. "Neither one of you followed any rules."

"There aren't any rules when you're trying to kill each other."

She shivered, looking at him, thinking how tough he could be, yet she knew there was another side to him.

They drove to the hospital and he insisted they look at her jaw. She was given an ice pack and then she waited while they checked Colin, taped his broken ribs and stitched up his temple. They went from the hospital to the sheriff's office to give their statements.

Finally Katherine drove Colin home. They entered a lit kitchen and Katherine saw a note propped on the kitchen table.

Dear Katherine and Colin,
Dad came to get me and we have taken Emily home with us. If it is all right, we would like to keep her all night. She can try out the new cradle Dad made for her. Give us a call when you get in.

Love,
Mom.

Katherine replaced the note. "Feel like calling her?"

"You do it. I don't feel like moving. I'm having a beer."

"How about a steak? I can put them on to broil."

"Sounds good." He walked over to her and placed his hands on her shoulders. "I thought I wasn't going to catch up with the two of you. It's a wonder I didn't roll the pickup."

"I told your mother not to page you."

"Well, Mom does her own thinking. You ought to be thankful."

"I am," she said. "I can't even kiss you. Your mouth looks like it hurts terribly."

"Try me," he said softly, so she did.

Hours later they had steaks and then Colin showed her that a man with broken ribs can still weave magic on the floor in front of the empty hearth.

The next morning she knew there was no reason to prolong the agony of parting. Colin knew his own mind and if he didn't want them in his life permanently, the sooner she left, the easier it would be for her and for Emily.

She dressed in jeans and a blue shirt and went to find him, thinking he would be at work. To her surprise, he was seated at the kitchen table. The sun was not yet up, the windows still dark, a cool breeze blowing through the open door. As she entered the kitchen, he came to his feet stiffly.

"I thought I tiptoed out quietly so you could sleep."

"I did sleep, and then I showered and then I packed."

Something flickered in the depths of his eyes, but he merely nodded. "Can I get you orange juice? Coffee?"

"Yes, orange juice please. No coffee," she replied, her gaze flicking over him, remembering their lovemaking, which had been so careful because of his broken ribs. His hair was caught in a strip of leather behind his head and his bruises had turned a dark blue. Even with cuts and bruises, he looked marvelous, and she watched him move around the kitchen, her gaze flicking over his broad shoulders, small waist and trim buttocks as she remembered how he had looked naked.

He turned and caught her studying him. She gave him a level look as he set down the orange juice and crossed the kitchen, his arm encircling her waist. He pulled her close, leaning down to kiss her slowly, a fiery possession that belied his cool manner.

Finally she pulled away, looking into his dark eyes while he seemed to be fighting some inner battle, and she wondered if he was struggling to control the yearnings of his heart. And she wished he was.

She moved away from him, barely aware of their conversation as she sat to eat breakfast. She loved him, this fierce, rugged man whose heart might as well be made of stone.

Finally she cleared the dishes with him and then reached for the phone to call the airlines. She found a flight that left at noon for San Francisco and she turned around as she replaced the phone. She prayed she could tell him in a steady voice without crying.

"I found a flight. It leaves at ten after twelve from Oklahoma City with a stopover in Phoenix."

"I'll take you. You're safe now, Katherine. When I think about you and Emily, I'll know you're safe." He walked to her to wrap his arms around her. "God, I'm going to miss you!" he said, his dark eyes telling her it went deeper than merely missing her.

He kissed her and carried her to bed, loving her long and slowly, a bittersweet hour that tore at her heart.

As they moved in unison, passion carrying them beyond feeling anything else, she cried out his name. "Colin! I love you. I will always love you!"

She was caught in a dizzying spiral, knowing she was reaffirming giving her heart to him, aware she was losing him at the same time. A climax made her spasm and cling to him, her hips thrusting against his as his body shuddered with release. When they calmed, he held her tightly. "I'll miss you."

She stroked his head and back and held him. *Say you want me to stay. Say it, Colin.*

But the words didn't come and she rose and showered and dressed. At nine o'clock they drove to his parents' place to get Emily and tell them goodbye.

As they headed toward the highway, Katherine felt numb. She didn't know what she said to him during the drive to the city. All she knew was that she was finally losing him and that she loved him beyond belief. And he hadn't revealed he felt anything until she noticed his knuckles on the steering wheel were white and a muscle continually worked in his jaw. And when his dark eyes focused on her, it was like gazing into the heat of a blast furnace. In those minutes, she felt wanted. She wanted to shout at him to let go and love again, but she clamped her mouth shut, knowing it was Colin's decision.

Finally they stood at the gate and he kissed her goodbye and then he turned swiftly, taking Emily from her and kissing her, holding her tightly in his arms. Katherine fought her tears as she looked at him and saw the silvery tears on his dark lashes, which made her shake. *Stubborn, stubborn man.*

Colin held Emily and he hurt so badly all over. He handed her back to Katherine and watched them give their boarding pass to the attendant and enter the jetway. Katherine's long red hair swung with each step and Emily was held on her shoulder, her tiny head showing, her wide blue eyes focused on him. He wanted to run after them and pull them back and yet he stood rooted, knowing that in minutes they would be gone and he would finally fall back into the routine he had known before they came along.

"Sir?"

The attendant was looking at him questioningly and he turned away, wiping his eyes. He hurt, and it was as bad a hurt as he had felt when he lost Dana.

He swore silently. Why did it hurt so damned much?
He shouldn't be that much in love with the woman. He
watched the jetway pull away from the plane. They were
on the plane, the doors were closed, they were flying out
of his life. He wanted to beat on the glass and call them
back. Be sensible, he told himself. All morning, he could
have stopped her. He hadn't wanted to risk his heart, but
the hurt he was feeling now told him that he had already
risked his heart and had just dealt himself a fatal blow by
letting them go.

He watched the plane turn from the airport and in
minutes it was gone from sight. He jammed his hands into
his pockets and left, climbing into his car and heading
north out of the lot. He felt as if his heart had been torn
out and he wondered if he hadn't just made the biggest
mistake of his life.

He slowed at a stop and turned to look over his shoulder.
"I think I made a mistake in letting you go. I want you
both."

Eleven

The plane gained speed, then lifted and was airborne, climbing swiftly and banking, the noon sun high overhead in a bright blue sky. Katherine wiped her eyes and jiggled Emily, who was fussing as if she sensed her mother's unhappiness.

Katherine settled Emily into the infant carrier, which she had buckled into the seat beside her, and looked out the window at the green landscape. Summer would come and Colin would work on his ranch and she would go on with her life.

She didn't want to go on with her life without him. He would have been a wonderful father for Emily. And he loved them, or he wouldn't have been shedding tears when they left. He wouldn't have loved her with the desperation he'd shown that morning, when he had stroked and kissed every inch of her.

She hurt and she couldn't stop crying, and she wished

she had just grabbed him and shaken him and asked him if he was sure about what he was doing.

Katherine continued to look at the land below, knowing every minute she was going farther and farther from him. All because this man who was so tough and brave was scared to risk getting hurt again. But he was already hurting.

Katherine shifted restlessly in the seat. He loved her. He had shown it in a hundred ways, risked his life for her, said he loved her. Why was she flying away from him as swiftly as she could?

She leaned over to stroke Emily's fine hair. "Maybe we should talk to him again," she whispered. "He loves us. We know that. His parents love us. All that stands in the way is this notion he has."

She looked at her watch. She had an hour stopover in Phoenix. Their whole future was at stake. Why go out to California and struggle with a life for Emily and herself when her heart was still back in Oklahoma? Why indeed, when the man she loved was shedding tears over telling her goodbye?

She studied Emily while her thoughts churned and she moved again, suddenly no longer able to sit still. The time seemed to crawl past until they finally announced Phoenix and the plane descended and landed, turning toward the Phoenix airport, where palms were swaying and the sun was hot.

Gathering Emily and her things, Katherine walked with a determined step as she went to the ticket counter.

"How soon can I get a flight to Oklahoma?"

Twelve

At one o'clock the following afternoon, Katherine landed in Oklahoma City. Disembarking from the plane, she took the escalator to a lower level and the car-rental desk.

Over an hour later she slowed on the drive to Will Whitefeather's house. Nadine stepped out the back door. Wearing jeans and a T-shirt, her long hair in a braid down her back, she stood watching Katherine slow and get out.

She crossed the yard to the car. "You came back," she said, her voice filled with joy. "Is Colin with you?" she asked, peering around Katherine at the car.

"No, he's not. Would you keep Emily for a while? I decided to come back and talk to Colin one more time."

Nadine looked at Katherine, who gazed back steadfastly, and then Nadine smiled and held out her arms, hugging Katherine. "I'm glad. He needs you."

"I'm not sure he knows that," Katherine said.

Nadine passed her and went to the car. "Here's my little

girl. Come to Nana, sweetie. I always wanted a little girl. Now I'll have two," she said, leaning into the car to get Emily. She unbuckled her and lifted the baby into her arms. "I'll keep her as long as you like. Tomorrow, next week—don't come back until the stubborn man stops acting so foolish."

Laughing, Katherine rushed around the car. "I'll bring her things." She carried Emily's belongings inside and set them in the front room. "You're sure?"

"Go on. You're wasting time here."

"Thank you. I may be back very soon."

"I don't think so," Nadine said, smoothing Emily's fine hair and kissing the top of her head. "We'll have a fun time today, won't we?"

Katherine left, closing the back door, hurrying to the car. Every mile, her tension heightened. All the bleak possibilities assaulted her: she might not be able to find him. He would send her rushing back to the airport. He had left the ranch and no one would know where to find him.

She drove to the house and knocked at the back door. When no one answered, she climbed back into the car and drove slowly past the garage and down to the barn. She spotted him then. Wearing faded jeans and a T-shirt, he was bending over, rolling up baling wire. He glanced around and straightened to watch her.

Her pulse drummed and her palms felt sweaty. She flushed and felt foolish and wondered if this was going to be one of the worst moments of her life or one of the best. She drove up beside him and opened the door. "C'mon, get in. This time I can protect you. I can keep you from getting hurt."

He pushed his hat to the back of his head, dropped a piece of baling wire and walked over to the open door of the car. He placed his hands on the car and leaned down.

"What are you doing?"

"A long time ago I took you up on your offer for protection. I took a risk then. Now I think it's time you risk that tin heart of yours, Colin. Get in. Nothing's going to take me away from you. And I don't want to go through life missing you."

She looked into his dark eyes and held her breath. He straightened and walked around the car. For a moment she wondered if he was going to send her packing, and she thought she would curl up and die on the spot. He opened her door. "Get out."

Still holding her breath, she stepped out. His hand closed around her wrist. "Come here, Katherine."

She rushed along with him as he took her around the corner into the barn and then closed the big doors behind him. "Colin?" Her heart began to pound while she watched him.

He turned around, his gaze burning as it went over her slowly. He crossed to her to swing her up into his arms and head for one of the empty stalls.

"What are you doing?"

"Taking you up on your offer," he said in a husky voice.

"In the barn? Someone will come—"

"I locked the doors." He set her on her feet and stood looking down at her beneath the broad brim of his hat. He bent down to kiss her, winding his arm around her waist and pulling her up against him.

Her heart thudded, while amazement and joy and desire fanned white-hot in her. *He wanted her to stay.* It had been so easy after all.

Colin shifted slightly and his fingers worked free the buttons of her shirt and he pushed it away. He unfastened the clasp of her bra and cupped her breasts, bending his head to flick his tongue over her nipple, feeling the tight bud.

Joyous, she tossed his hat away, running her fingers in his hair.

Colin's heart pounded, and all he could think was that she was here. She was back, and he heard the challenge she had made and the offer she had given and he knew what he wanted. He could feel the final barriers crumbling. Katherine was special, a very special woman, and he had already risked his heart. He knew he needed to tell her, to let her know what he felt, but at the moment all he could do was kiss and love her. He wanted to possess her, to drive her to the fiery passion that would consume them both. Later he would tell her, later after love...

He slid his hands along the curve of her back and down over her bottom, pulling her up against him. Then he turned her, so he could get to the buttons of her jeans and push them away.

She caught his hands. "I came back for a reason."

"I know you did," he said, his dark eyes seeming to pierce to her soul. She inhaled, her heart thudding at the look of need in his expression and then his mouth covered hers in a white-hot kiss that claimed possession. She returned his kiss, feeling his hands removing clothing, knowing their lovemaking wasn't solving anything.

He shoved her down in the straw, moving between her legs, pausing over her. He was dark, powerful, aroused. Her heart ached with love for him and she slipped her legs up along his thighs, locking them around him to pull him down.

He entered her in a hard thrust, taking her and covering her mouth as he moved so slowly, withdrawing and then sliding into her again, driving her wild as sensations shot through her like summer lightning streaking across a night sky.

A storm of passion swept her up and she clung to his lean body, moving with him, hearts pounding together. It was wild and mindless and right. She had come home and she wasn't leaving unless he bodily carried her away. And then she cried out her love and his name over and over.

When they climaxed, she dimly heard him cry her name hoarsely. "Katherine, love!"

His weight finally came down on her and she held him tightly. Satiated, damp, she held him while passion changed to determination.

"Colin, I'm not going to walk out and leave what we have behind. If I have to fight you—"

"I know, love. Marry me."

"You're a warmhearted person—" She realized what he had just said to her and she twisted to look at him, seeing dark eyes that studied her intently.

"Marry me, Katherine," he said in a husky voice. "I shouldn't have let you go."

Her heart missed beats and she stared at him. "You really want to marry me?"

His dark brows drew together like thunderclouds gathering. "Why did you come back?"

"To marry you."

"I think we're talking in circles. So you'll marry me."

"Yes," she gasped, closing her eyes, realizing he really meant it. "You'll take all those risks of loving?" Her eyes flew open to meet his level gaze.

"I think I started loving you the night I delivered Emily."

"A declaration of love or commitment is what I wanted when I stopped and opened the car door. I didn't expect a tumble in the hay. And it's scratchy," she said, wiggling against him.

He grinned and kissed her throat. "I made plane reservations this morning to fly to San Francisco next Saturday."

"Did you really?" she asked, her pulse jumping. She

wound her arms around his neck. "I'm glad. Now I know you made that decision and I didn't just strong-arm you into marriage."

"Oh, yes, you did. Strong-armed isn't the right description. Maybe seduced would fit better," he said, kissing her throat and trailing kisses to her mouth. She turned her head to kiss him and he wrapped his arms tightly around her.

She pulled back after a few minutes to look at him solemnly. "I love you, Colin. Always."

"I've loved you for a long time. I just had to let go of my fears."

"That should have been my line. You vanquished all my fears so quickly before Emily was born and that night when you delivered her. There's never been anything since then except love."

"Let's marry soon. And we can take a short wedding trip. I know who will keep Emily. And I imagine that's where she is right now."

"You're right. Your mother said she would keep her as long as I wanted. Today, tomorrow—but I'm not staying in this hay—"

"That's what you think, lady," he said gruffly, bending to kiss her, and her words were lost as he stirred up the storm of passion that shut out the world.

Later while he held her, he stroked her back. "Thank heaven you came back. I heard a car motor and looked around and couldn't believe my eyes. I had missed you so badly, for a moment I thought I was hallucinating."

"I want to hear again about your missing me."

His dark eyes were intense on her and she saw the yearning that was unmistakable. "I wanted you constantly, mindlessly, passionately. Notice, this time when we made love, I didn't insist on any infernal protection, which you have fought every time."

"I noticed, sort of. We have to get our act together—

now I'm on the Pill. Maybe someday we can give Emily a little brother or little sister. Now about missing us—''

"I missed you unbearably. I love you and Emily with all my heart and I shouldn't have let you go. I missed you every minute, and I wanted to fling myself out the door of the airport and run after your plane. It's been hell without you.''

"Colin," she breathed, letting go of the last doubt. She wrapped her arms more tightly around him, knowing his heart had mended and they would be a family and she would have the love of a wonderful man. Smiling she pulled him close. "Colin, my love," she whispered. She had finally come home.

*　*　*　*　*

FANTASTIC NEWS!

For all you devoted Diana Palmer fans
Silhouette Books is pleased to bring you
a brand-new novel and short story by one of the
top ten romance writers in America

"Nobody tops Diana Palmer...I love her stories."
—*New York Times* bestselling author
Jayne Ann Krentz

**Diana Palmer has written another thrilling desire.
Man of the Month Ramon Cortero was a talented
surgeon, existing only for his work—until the
night he saved nurse Noreen Kensington's life. But
their stormy past makes this romance a challenge!**

THE PATIENT NURSE
Silhouette Desire
October 1997

And in November Diana Palmer adds to the
Long, Tall Texans series with *CHRISTMAS COWBOY*, in
LONE STAR CHRISTMAS, a fabulous new holiday
keepsake collection by talented authors Diana Palmer
and Joan Johnston. Their heroes are seductive,
shameless and irresistible—and these Texans are
experts at sneaking kisses under the mistletoe! So get
ready for a sizzling holiday season....

Only from *Silhouette*®

Take 4 bestselling love stories FREE

Plus get a FREE surprise gift!

Special Limited-time Offer

Mail to Sihouette Reader Service™

> P.O. Box 609
> Fort Erie, Ontario
> L2A 5X3

YES! Please send me 4 free Silhouette Desire® novels and my free surprise gift. Then send me 6 brand-new novels every month, which I will receive months before they appear in bookstores. Bill me at the low price of $3.24 each plus 25¢ delivery and GST*. That's the complete price and a savings of over 10% off the cover prices—quite a bargain! I understand that accepting the books and gift places me under no obligation ever to buy any books. I can always return a shipment and cancel at any time. Even if I never buy another book from Silhouette, the 4 free books and the surprise gift are mine to keep forever.

326 BPA A3UY

Name	(PLEASE PRINT)	
Address	Apt. No.	
City	Province	Postal Code

This offer is limited to one order per household and not valid to present Silhouette Desire® subscribers. *Terms and prices are subject to change without notice. Canadian residents will be charged applicable provincial taxes and GST.

CDES-696

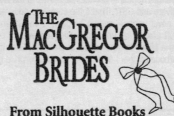
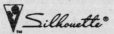

National Bestselling Author

MARY LYNN BAXTER

"Ms. Baxter's writing...strikes every chord within the female spirit."
—Sandra Brown

LONE STAR
Heat

SHE is Juliana Reed, a prominent broadcast journalist whose television show is about to be syndicated. Until the murder...

HE is Gates O'Brien, a high-ranking member of the Texas Rangers, determined to forget about his ex-wife. He's onto something bad....

Juliana and Gates are ex-spouses, unwillingly involved in an explosive circle of political corruption, blackmail and murder.

In order to survive, they must overcome the pain of the past...and the very demons that drove them apart.

Available in September 1997 at your favorite retail outlet.

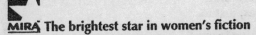

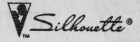

DIANA WHITNEY

**Continues the twelve-book
series 36 HOURS in
September 1997
with Book Three**

OOH BABY, BABY

In the back of a cab, in the midst of a disastrous storm,
Travis Stockwell delivered Peggy Saxon's two precious babies
and, for a moment, they felt like a family. But Travis was a
wandering cowboy, and a fine woman like Peggy was better off
without him. Still, she and her adorable twins had tugged on
his heartstrings, until now he wasn't so sure that *he* was
better off without *her.*

For Travis and Peggy and *all* the residents of Grand Springs,
Colorado, the storm-induced blackout was just the beginning
of 36 Hours that changed *everything!* You won't want to miss a
single book.

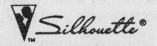